UNEASY LIES

by

Eve Zaremba

SECOND STORY Press

FEMINIST
PUBLISHERS

For Ottie
and The Carnivores

CANADIAN CATALOGUING IN PUBLICATION DATA

Zaremba, Eve
Uneasy lies

ISBN 0-929005-17-1
I Title.
PS8599.A74U54 1990   C813'.54   C90-095066-8
PR9199.3.Z37U54 1990

Second Story Press gratefully acknowledges the assistance of the
Ontario Arts Council.

Printed and Bound in Canada

Published by
SECOND STORY PRESS
760 Bathurst Street
Toronto Canada M5S 2R6

4

ALICE SAYS I'M A LOUSY PASSENGER and she's right. But this time I felt justified. My cabbie didn't know his way. This Metro Toronto taxi driver had apparently never been north of Highway 401. And there's a lot of city north of the 401. Much of it goes by the name of North York, but that doesn't fool anyone. It's still Toronto. As it was, I had to sit in the cab, watching the back of his neck, listening to him mutter, "Braemore, Baymore, Braemount ..."

There are few of life's minor inconveniences more annoying than being driven round in circles by an incompetent with dandruff.

"It's Braymount. B-R-A-Y-M-O-U-N-T," I told him for the tenth time.

It did not help that I wasn't sure I really wanted to get to our destination. By the time we finally found the unlisted street in the brand new development and drove up the freshly paved semicircular drive leading to the bulky up-to-the-minute tower, which reared up over fancy glass doors, I would rather have been some other place.

Twenty-eight hundred Braymount Avenue would be better known to readers of the real estate pages as "DIAMOND PLAZA TOWERS, Exclusive Condominium Residences for the Discriminating. Phase I sold out. Priority registration for Phase II: Inquire Sales Office at 883-1111." At the edge of the property, a large tastefully lettered sign listed all the wonderful people who were making big money building, designing, financing, marketing, and managing this latest in Toronto's condominiums — for which we should all be duly grateful.

The recently landscaped grounds fronting the Towers didn't help my mood. They had all the rustic charm of a diagram in a landscaping manual. You could just about see the ruled lines, the pencil shadings. Not a blade of grass out of place; not a twig an inch longer than plans called for. Horizontal junipers here, pyramid yews there; foundation planting with weeping mulberry; the ubiquitous dogwoods, forsythia, and decorative dwarf trees in one corner, young shade trees in another. A fountain, and something I am sure they call a gazebo, to make it formal. And of course a few strategically placed limestone rocks torn out of the Niagara Escarpment, for that touch of class. All set down with military precision, and surrounded by fancy decorative wrought-iron fencing. Nature kept under perfect control at all times and not allowed to run wild, upsetting the discriminating owners of these exclusive residences.

I walked past the row of intercom buzzers, coyly coded with numbers instead of names, and pushed the second set of double doors. A buzzer sounded; the doors swung open automatically. Inside more "no surprises." A cavernous lobby, complete with chandeliers and maroon carpet. More maroon on a wall hanging, with an indistinct diamond pattern picked out in brown. Leather couch and armchairs on which nobody would ever relax, glass coffee tables which would never see a coffee cup. Set to one side was the pièce de résistance of every luxury-condo lobby — a large security desk. A U-shaped counter, with a double bank of video monitors overlooking an impressive control panel with more switches, buttons, and lights than a 757 cockpit.

And this was to be mine, all mine for six glorious weeks! I could hardly wait.

A pleasant-faced security guard in a maroon blazer with a diamond-shaped DP embroidered on the pocket directed me to the administration office. There, a secretarial type in mufti showed me the door to the manager's office. And inside was Clare Harwood, sitting behind a utilitarian desk, chewing her nails.

"Hi, Helen! Glad you made it. I was afraid you would change your mind," Clare greeted me effusively. She was a short, energetic Anglo, with carefully arranged hair, dressed in a businesslike shirtwaist dress of bright blue. No maroon in her office ...

"I said I would come and so here I am. Against my better judgement, mind you ... I guess you talked me into it."

I was being ungracious and knew it. Clare was too happy and relieved to see me to notice.

"You'll be glad you agreed, just wait and see. Consider it a vacation with pay. A snap of a job for you, for someone with your experience. And you'll be doing me a great favour. I appreciate this, really I do. I don't know what I would have done if we hadn't met at the Common yesterday. Real lucky break. And you being free and all! Solves all my problems, and helps you, too. Come on, Helen, admit it!"

"Well, I guess. It'll keep me out of pool halls, anyway. I was getting squirrelly just hanging around this town. Don't much like not having anything to do and no place of my own to do it in. Now that I am here, let's get on with this. You want me to sub for your house dick, right? Six weeks, a thousand dollars per, plus car and apartment. Sounds like money for old rope, all right. What's the catch? Your house dick will be away for six weeks? Kind of long for a vacation. How come you need a replacement at such short notice? Fill me in. You got problems?"

"House dick! What an idea! Head of security, please, Helen!" Clare laughed. "He's got a family emergency, and since it's in India he was allowed six weeks unpaid leave of absence. And the problem? The problem is that I'll be away for the first three weeks of the six. And Wayne, that's the assistant manager, is only twenty-five. I cannot leave him alone, to cover for both me and Nicky."

The picture was becoming clearer. I was being hired to babysit.

"Nicky who?"

"Nikhil Das. Head of security. He's Indian, East Indian I mean. Naturally we call him Nicky. He will show you around presently. We're very proud of our security system. State of the art, you know."

"Bully for you! Okay, so he'll show me all the bells and whistles. What else do you want from me? What else should I know?"

"Well, you must meet Wayne Tillion, like I said, he's the assistant manager. This is his first responsible job. He's keen and bright. So be nice. Don't come on too heavy with him. Remember, he's just a kid. He will sub for me and you'll sub for Nicky and, with luck, no big problem will crop up while I am away. Just keep everything at status quo ... "

Clare went on to tell me what she thought I needed to know. Names, places, routines, no-no's, forms, keys. I listened with half an ear, on automatic pilot, thinking about my previous encounters with Clare Harwood.

Some dozen years before, Clare and I had had a brief encounter of the lustful kind. She had come out with someone she'd met at the Michigan Women's Music Festival, and there had been no stopping her after that. She was young and ardent and I was experienced and available. It had been nice while it lasted but it hadn't lasted long. When it was over, we parted friends. As I recalled, at the time she had just left her husband — or he had left her — and was alone with two young kids, little money, few skills, and no prospects.

Now, years later, here she was sitting behind a desk in a room with Manager on the door, hiring me to look after her boy-assistant.

I guess I should have stayed in Alice's little sublet near Spadina and College. Or at least not allowed myself to be conned into coming here. Sitting at the Women's Common the night before, trying to decide whether to stay and have another drink or go somewhere else and have another drink, I had found Clare a welcome distraction. Cashing in on our status as ex-lovers, no matter how fleeting and distant in time, she moved in to schmooze. Got me to admit that I was at loose ends in Toronto, only hanging around because Alice Caplan was here trying to break into Toronto's theatre scene.

Clare immediately offered to buy me another drink — she herself still didn't indulge — and probed for more about Alice. By then my moment of weakness was over and I clammed up on her. So she went on to ask whether I wanted a job. Just for six weeks, good pay, no sweat. I was tired of walking the streets and staring at the apartment walls, waiting for Alice to get back from some rehearsal or other. So I said yes, I'll do it, I'll solve your problem, I'll come to Diamond Plaza

Towers, I'll take the job ... Now that I wished I hadn't, it was too late.

Reluctantly I switched back to what Clare was saying.

"You'd better see Wayne first, before Nicky takes you around. Just so he doesn't have any reason to feel slighted."

I wondered about this kid assistant manager who had to be handled with such care.

Clare picked up the phone and, a few moments later, in walked Wayne Tillion, an unexceptional-looking young man whose most salient feature was a prominent Adam's apple. He was neatly dressed in an uninspired but well-pressed suit and looked quite grown-up, as I was relieved to note. Clare introduced me — "Wayne, this is Helen Keremos, she'll be taking Nicky's place while he's away" — and went on to explain my status at Diamond Plaza Towers, using more words than were strictly necessary.

Tillion managed to do a fair job of hiding his dismay once my role had been made clear. But a shock it was, nonetheless. The sudden appearance of a middle-aged lady dick, when probably he had expected to run the place alone during Clare's absence, was not welcome at all, at all.

"Tough break, my man," I said, but only to myself.

Clare continued to wax managerial while Wayne Tillion and I shook hands and took each other's measure. On eye contact it was silently established that the next tussle between us would wait until Clare had left, so he and I could square off without having to take her into account. The situation had possibilities.

"I am sure Wayne and I will get along just fine," I lied through my teeth. "Now, better get Mr. Das to brief me on this state-of-the-art security setup of yours. And I'd like to see the apartment I am getting ..."

"Ah, yes, I am afraid that will be Nicky's apartment, he's agreed you can use it while he's away. We don't really have any staff apartments other than the head of security. It's on the second floor, quite nice, cleaners come in twice a week, I am sure you'll like it. After all, it's only for six weeks," Clare said, all in one breath. From one sublet to another, I thought with resignation. "And a car, of course you'll have the use of Nicky's company vehicle. A Ford," Clare continued.

"An Escort, to be exact." Wayne looked pleased to be able to provide this detail. I bet he didn't drive an Escort. He looked like a Firebird man to me.

"Ford Escort will be fine. Wheels are wheels." I said, refusing to prolong this encounter.

Clare reached for the phone again. Wayne excused himself and I waited for the man whose job, apartment, and automobile I was to take over for the next six weeks.

▲

NIKHIL "NICKY" DAS, HEAD OF SECURITY of Diamond Plaza Towers, was a stocky man in his forties who spoke upper-class British English with a slight Anglo-Indian accent. He wore grey slacks, well-shined shoes, a tweed jacket, and what looked liked a regimental tie. He was professional, unhurried, and courteous. A man to be reckoned with.

Sitting in his tiny office off the lobby, just around the corner from the main security desk, we talked first about his job.

The much vaunted state-of-the-art security turned out to be the standard garden variety system sold expensively to any number of condominium developments. It featured an outside alarm, which on being tripped took over the phone line and signalled the main security desk plus the nearest police station. I asked about false alarms. About two per week were standard, Nicky told me, smiling. "Nothing but a nuisance."

Then there were the mandatory video cameras in all public areas and exits: in the elevators, the roof, at each emergency exit, underground garage, doors into the health complex, in the entrance to tennis and squash courts, swimming pool, change rooms. All together sixty-four cameras, some running full time and some motion activated, with sixteen monitors at the main security station, that is the desk in the lobby, each covering four locations. Plus one master monitor, which could be switched to any input, right there in the office where we sat.

"We have two staff on duty at all times, at least one must stay at the desk. They are supposed to check visitors in and out, help residents, answer questions, take deliveries, watch for strangers hanging about … *and* watch sixteen of these little grey video monitors. Have you spent any time looking at these things? Sends you cross-eyed and dulls the mind. After a while you don't know what you're seeing, if anything," Das told me.

"But no condo development would be complete without them."

"Exactly. Plus, there is a fire alarm system hard-wired into all this, smoke detectors, temperature monitors, utility system breakdown detectors, vibration and sound discriminators — God knows what else."

"How much of this do you think is really necessary in a security sense?" I asked finally.

"Very little. Helen, I'll be frank. This isn't a high crime area. The only real problem spot might be the underground garage. And there are simpler ways of handling that. Of course a good fire alarm system is necessary, but apart from that, realistically, all we need is a couple of smart concierge types who know their job — which is primarily to service the residents. That is all. I don't think a place like this needs a live-in head of security with a staff which is trained in security and not service. That makes a difference, as you are well aware. And we certainly don't require a couple of hundred thousand dollars worth of gadgets. But people expect all this and are willing to pay for it. So it's supplied."

"What's the appeal?" I probed.

"Well, I call it the world-class syndrome. People in cities like Toronto are prone to it. You have to act as if under constant siege, otherwise how will you be sure you are big time?"

We laughed together. Bright guy this Nicky Das, I thought as we left his office to see in action all this expensive technology and the staff who ran it.

In short order I met the security personnel on duty: Selena Amos and Raphael Clementi, with their neat maroon blazers, professional coolness, and bored eyes. On our way down to inspect the garage we ran across Sam Feng, the security supervisor. Das made the introductions. As his second in command, Feng would continue to run the operation, staff scheduling and routine details of the system. He didn't make any particular impression on me at the time, but since he did all the real work, meeting him did leave me wondering just what my role was to be.

Phase I of Diamond Plaza Towers had only been completed

six months previously. All the suites had been sold, presold in fact, but not all were currently occupied. We walked past the elevators, down the short flight of stairs, and through the fire door to the basement, with Das pointing out cameras which constantly monitored this, the most vulnerable area.

The garage area smelled new, of concrete and paint, rather than gas fumes and spilled oil, as it would very soon. Nicky Das led me past the fifty or so automobiles parked in well-marked spaces along the concrete walls. He had given me a numbered list of garage spaces, with all cars by model and licence cross-referenced to names and apartment numbers of residents. In the office we had already examined a master list of residents, with these data in reverse. Automatically I was registering information which my conscious mind did not see as of much importance. Any job, even a routine six-week locum, was more interesting when done well. There was no harm in getting to know whom and what I had been hired to serve and protect.

In spite of all the hype, DP Towers was not full of million-aires. Just people managing to get by on eighty thousand dollars or so a year. Types and models of cars, not to mention their vanity plates, are a dead give-away of the status of any residential development. At Diamond Plaza Towers about half the cars were upscale Japanese sedans in neutral shades, totally indistinquishable from each other. Who can tell a Legend from a Legacy; who wants to? Among them lurked a few much polished BMW's and Audis, a number of North American minivans, woody station wagons and full-sized sedans, one Suzuki Sidekick, one beat-up Olds, a couple of sporty muscle cars, noses to the ground and tails in the air, a lone Thunderbird, and a SAAB, (Turbo, of course). All sadly predictable and dull.

The only anomalies seemed to be a rusty Dakota pickup on

the downscale side, and on the upscale a handsome white Jaguar XJS with blue interior. Next to the Jaguar stood the only convertible in the bunch; a white Chrysler LeBaron with red interior. Something drew my attention to the licence plates: "FLOSSS" ordered the Jaguar's, "FLOSSY" said the convertible's.

"I guess dentists have to have their fun, too," I said to Das, out of curiosity looking down the list. With no surprise I found that both the Jag and the little ragtop belonged to Suite 1609, to Dr. Melhior Romulu and Ms. Eleena DeMoulard respectively. Das grimaced and said, "It's all quite amusing, I dare say. Dr. Romulu is indeed a dentist and the young lady is … a friend of his. They occupy a double suite, are well mannered, and give no trouble."

Short and not too sweet. The hint of disapproval in his voice was barely noticeable. In his own way, Nikhil Das was a snob. I promised myself to find out more about Melhior and Eleena — what juicy names — and perhaps make an effort to meet them. It would help pass the time at Diamond Plaza, time of which I was sure I would have more than enough.

I made no further comment as we moved on to the garage exit where a ramp led up to a solid overhead door controlled from the inside by vehicle-sensitive motion sensors and a coded card system from the outside. All perfectly standard issue security. I took my time examining the override mechanism for the door, in a locked box at the bottom of the ramp. Das had already handed over a very serious bunch of keys, and I knew there was a whole rack of them in his office.

"What about other exits from the building, including the basement level? Building codes demand exits, so does the fire marshal. How do you control mandatory emergency exits which cannot be kept locked?"

"That is a problem. All we can do is to have visual surveillance and an alarm system on all the emergency exits. When any of these doors is used, even if it's opened only a crack, the camera is activated and a signal alerts the staff at the main desk that security has been breached. Usually it's just one of the maintenance crew. He will wave at the camera and my staff will ignore it. Some residents like using these doors as a shortcut to the grounds. We try to wean them of that but it's hard. Bulk of our false alarms are caused by unauthorized use of emergency doors."

Having exhausted for the moment the entertainment possibilities of the garage and the "state-of-the-art" security system, we made our way via the elevator to the second floor and Apartment 211, which I was expected to occupy for the next six weeks.

▲

"SCOTCH?" DAS HELD UP two heavy cut-glass highball glasses, pouring out a good two ounces of single malt whisky into one, presumably for himself. I nodded and he filled the second one. I was being treated as an equal, a gentleman of taste. It was a compliment and meant to be taken as such.

Scotch isn't my drink and I am hardly a gentleman by any possible definition. Still, I accepted this treatment without protest. Das had found the only way he could comfortably treat me as a professional colleague. It was common courtesy, as well as sense, to let him.

We sipped our drinks in silence. I looked around the small apartment, one of only two such one-bedrooms in the DP complex. Das had already given me the brief tour mandatory on such occasions. Politely I had inspected the militarily austere bedroom, blanket on the single bed tight with hospital corners; the tiny awkwardly designed bathroom smelling of expensive aftershave; the galley kitchen with full-sized refrigerator, stove, and dishwasher packed together in the space of a closet.

Now we sat in the living room, with our backs to the dining area, facing a large window and door to the balcony which overlooked the staff parking lot. The room contained a black leather sofa and armchair set, a small coffee table, a compact Technics radio/CD player, and one full wall of bookshelves, probably from Ikea. I checked out the books with pardonable curiosity since I was to live with them for six weeks. Apart from a shelf or two of books in — I assumed — Hindi, they were English. A mixed lot of popular works on World War II, heavy on British and Indian military and regimental histories and biographies of generals. Some travel books by well-known people like Morris, Theroux, Naipaul, and Chatwin. And surprisingly a much-read selection of memoirs and novels of the Raj by Brits from Kipling to Paul Scott. I guess it was history to him, too. From the looks of their spines, very few were recent or bought locally. There were certainly lots I hadn't read and only a few I was interested to try.

"I hear you're off to India on a family emergency. Nothing too serious, I hope," I said, judging the time ripe for a tactful inquiry.

"Serious enough. My brother-in-law had been very, very ill, not expected to live. So I made plans to go home and be with my sister. And indeed today I received notice of his death. It's just as well that I will be there for the funeral. And of course there will be arrangements to be made for my sister and her children."

"Ah, I am sorry. Are you close to your in-laws?"

"No, I am close to my sister," he said, and fell silent.

Any further questions would constitute prying. My language stilted and uncomfortable, I said, "Well, I hope you have a good trip and that all goes as well as possible under the circumstances. You have been very helpful and I hope you'll find everything shipshape when you get back. Oh, and thanks for the whisky."

"Not at all, not at all. It's been a pleasure. I should get on with my packing, otherwise I would love to have you dine with me." A polite brush-off.

"I understand. I'm on my way. Before I go there is a question I hope you can answer without being indiscreet. Just what's the scoop on Wayne Tillion? And how would you advise I handle him?"

"Wayne Tillion? Oh, my! Just a boy, you know. Clare babies him rather, not good for a young man. But you shouldn't have any problems with him. He doesn't have much to do with our work. Feng will deal with whatever needs to be dealt with, anyway."

"If Feng will deal with everything, what am I needed for, may I ask?"

"Well, quite frankly I am not sure I know. It's Clare's decision, she's the manager. Still, I expect she checked with HQ, and Mr. Glendenning advised her not to leave young Tillion on his own."

"Who's Glendenning?" I asked, exasperated. Das' answer had left me no further ahead as far as my role vis-à-vis Tillion and Feng was concerned.

"Mr. Glendenning is the head of Diamond Development Corporation, the company which built and now manages Diamond Plaza Towers. He's the commanding officer, as it were. Incidentally, I belive he's some relative of young Tillion. Uncle, possibly."

Incidentally, the man says!

▲

AFTER THE RELATIVELY WIDE-OPEN spaces of north Toronto, Spadina south of College Street felt cozily urban. It was noisy with George Brown College kids and streetcars and smelly with gasoline fumes and rotting vegetables from nearby Kensington Market. For the past few weeks I had enjoyed the street life here, but now it felt good to leave.

Alice had taken the news of my new job and imminent departure very well. Too well. Not that I wanted any trouble in that department, but who isn't a bit miffed when her lover accepts separation without apparent regrets?

"Great that you've found a job and with an apartment yet. Even if it's in the burbs. You've been climbing the walls around here, with nothing to do and me away so much. Be better for both of us." That's what she'd said, word for word, on arriving home late that night, tired and full of her own theatrical affairs.

Alice Caplan is scathing about suburbs, having spent the first fifteen years of her life in one. Burnaby, British Columbia, was no place for her. At twelve she wanted to be a ballerina, at fourteen a rock-and- roll performer, at fifteen she left home and made her way alone to L.A. and show biz, becoming one of the lost children advertised on milk cartons. Predictably, by sixteen she was on the street, with a case of herpes, a budding cocaine habit, and a bad-ass attitude. Except she didn't end up on the street. She looked around and saw that if she stayed tricking, her choice was either to get to like being a victim or to persuade herself she wasn't one. Alice had the brains to figure out that this wasn't much of a choice and the willpower to do something about it. Some of us are swifter than others, and Alice is nothing if not swift.

To cut a long tale short, she managed to shake off the street scene in L.A. and make it back to Canada, to school and Vancouver's fringe theatre. When I met her she was supporting her acting habit by working part time for my old friend Jessica Tsukada, a hot-shot lawyer. At one time Alice had actually started to study law! Then both Alice and Jessica got involved in one of my cases in the B.C. Interior, where we met a bunch of lesbian communards. When it was all over Alice stayed on the land with them for a season. But the acting bug was too strong. She was now single-mindedly pursuing her ambitions in Toronto while I mooned around. What can I say?

It was past time to be gone, at least out of this crummy apartment if not Alice's life altogether. Had I not met Clare that night at the club, it would have taken me a few more days or even weeks to figure this out. The DP Towers job was already having repercussions on my relationship and I wasn't even working at it yet.

So the morning after my first look at the Towers, I packed my duffle, kissed Alice, and walked down to the dirty blue Escort parked around the corner on Cecil Street. There was a yellow parking tag on it. No skin off my nose — it was a company car, let DP pay for it.

It was great to have wheels again. I've owned a car since high school in San Diego. My dad bought me the first one soon after I moved to the U.S. to live with him after my mother died. Since then I've never felt complete without one. This morning just muscling my way north against the morning traffic gave me a rush. Maybe that was part of my problem all along; I should have rented a car on arrival. Then I would have felt better about being here. Maybe now that I had one I could quit feeling sorry for myself, make it right with Alice and prolong our honeymoon. Maybe.

I didn't think I was ready to give up Alice. Alice was addictive. She had the athletic body of a dancer and a mind that saw around corners. She was serious and flighty, honest and devious, solid and flexible all at once. And she was a sexual choreographer of immense skill, imagination, and energy.

The first time we were together I woke up in the morning in a tangle of sticky sheets, barely able to move, and yearning to start all over again. On a mat next to me was Alice, fresh as spring, going through her morning stretches. I wasn't exactly new at this, but I had never before made love with anyone who could do the splits. Imagine!

For months after that first night we went on to wear ourselves out anywhere and any time, tearing at each other with an almost painful urgency, perpetually wearing silly grins along with yellowing bruises. Now I had to admit that my aging body was begining to feel the strain. It was no match for Alice's twenty-six-year-old stamina honed by hours of exercise. I am twice her age. I've been young and I've been not-so-young, and when it comes to sexual vigour, young is better. Believe it.

By the time the Escort hit Allen Road I had accepted that I was really and truly glad to be away from Alice and downtown Toronto, glad to have even a house-dick job. Much as I loved both Alice and the downtown scene, they were getting to me. Besides, it would be nice to be bored on someone else's time instead of my own.

▲

THAT FIRST DAY certainly lived up to my expectations. On a boredom scale of 1 to 5, it was about a 4.5. By the time I arrived, Nicky Das and Clare Harwood were both gone and I couldn't blame them for vacating the Towers as soon as they could. I spent the day wafting here and there, like a bad smell. After dumping my bag in Das' apartment, I tried to spend at least a couple of hours at his desk, going over the paperwork and getting familiar with the operation. But I couldn't make it stretch to more than ninety minutes. So I went out to lunch at nearby Yorkdale Mall, a plush high-hype operation catering to born-to-shoppers. After a drink and an expensive snack, I bought some groceries and wasted another hour window shopping, but still got back to the salt mines before two.

The rest of the afternoon I made myself obnoxious by sitting on one of the showy leather couches in the lobby, checking out the passing parade and watching the watchers at the security desk. The security staff studiously pretended I was invisible. Just as well the Jays weren't playing. I might have earned their undying hate for making them watch the garage doors and emergency exits on dull grey monitor screens instead of baseball on the little TV hidden under the desk. And I wouldn't have blamed them.

Not much happens on a weekday afternoon in a suburban condo lobby, and this place was no exception. Residents of DP Towers may not be working class, but most work. During office hours only a few, some retired couples and the rest mostly married women, are in the building. Of those, not many cross the lobby, since the elevators take them straight down to the garage and up again. So only those few pass through the lobby who actually walk anywhere and take the subway, plus those who use the health club or the little convenience store on the premises. And from the outside, the mail and most other deliveries arrive in the morning. So the afternoon is very dead. A dry cleaner with a stack of shirts and suits on hangers was as exciting as it got.

I was about to nod off when a lonely insurance adjuster arrived. He tried to get into the garage to examine a damaged automobile belonging to one of the absent residents, a Mr. Gurton. I watched the security staff deal with him and had to admit they showed some initiative, a rare quality in the breed. Gurton had not left them any instructions about the matter, and naturally the adjuster wasn't allowed in. However, it made sense that Gurton would blame the security staff and not himself for the consequent holdup in the insurance settlement, so Feng phoned his office to ask for instructions. It wasn't his fault that Gurton wasn't there. He then called Gurton's wife at her office and after some discussion got her okay to let the adjuster at the damaged auto. My opinion of Feng went up considerably. "Service," Das had said, and service is what the residents were getting. I wondered how many of them appreciated it.

At about four, Feng came over to me. He was small and neat, with an open, smiling face and regular Asian features. He was wearing his maroon blazer with pride. Would I like a cup of coffee? I would. He joined me and we sat and chatted. I congratulated him on his handling of the insurance adjuster. His face lit up with pleasure at the compliment. He doesn't get many, I bet.

"That's our job."

"How d'you like it?" I ask. "This job, I mean."

"Fine, just fine. Regular hours, well-run system. I can do good work here, be organized, like. Management knows what it's doing. That's good."

Interesting, I thought. Before I could draw Feng out some more, Tillion walked by. First he pretended not to see me, then did an obvious double take. We smiled at each other with palpable insincerity as he disappeared out the main door. I felt, more than saw, Feng relax. His body language was clear.

"How about Wayne Tillion, then? How good is he at his job?" I put a slight sneer into my voice and Feng rose to the bait.

"Him? About time he figured out what his job is. Assistant-manager trainee is what he's supposed to be. But all he does is snoop around and stick his nose where it doesn't belong. I don't know how Clare stands it, having him on her hands."

"Oh? So he's just a trainee, is he!"

"Well, that's what we were told when he arrived. A place like this doesn't need an assistant manager. When Phase II starts we will need sales reps, but an AM, no."

Just then a couple of teenage boys came slouching in, wheeling their bikes through the lobby towards the door leading to the health club and other facilities beyond, one of which is a bike storeroom.

One of the machines was a fancy mountain bike, probably worth the best part of a thousand dollars. Its owner had about that much on his back and feet in gaudy nothing-but-the-best gear. Black and neon-orange Spandex tights, NIKE cycling shoes, perforated mitts, and a leather backpack. Both he and his buddy looked to be a sulky and fast growing sixteen.

There were no small children here; DP Towers was promoted as an "adult lifestyle" building, meaning that people with children under fourteen are not welcome.

I lifted an eyebrow at Feng and grinned. He nodded and answered my unspoken question.

"Young Norman Dossler. His father died recently and their house was sold, so he and his mother moved in here."

"And thinks he's come down in the world, right?"

"Something like that. Acts a bit stuck-up. But an okay kid, no trouble." Feng gives his professional opinion.

"And the other?" I prompt. Feng frowns.

"He doesn't live here. A friend of Dossler's, I guess. I'll have to check on him."

"Check?"

"Well, it helps to know regular visitors. It's best if we know who he is, get the number of his bike, see if its okay with Mrs. Dossler to send him up any time. Things like that. That way we stay in control, like."

Control. I nodded and looked around. It's almost five and people were beginning to get back home from work or whatever. There was a bustle around the desk. Sam Feng left me without a word. Duty called. I had nothing to do but sit and watch the scene. Of course I could always just leave. No one would miss me. What the hell was I doing here?

▲

A CAN OF TUNA dumped into Lipton's instant pasta, heavily seasoned with Tamari and Jamaican hot sauce. That, plus a bottle of Upper Canada Ale, is my supper. Sitting eating it in Das' neat little pad watching first the six o'clock news on the CBC and then switching to "The MacNeil/Lehrer Newshour" on PBS, I can begin to relax and enjoy.

Living alone in someone else's home is comfortably familiar. I am good at it. First of all I am good at living alone, without anyone else's habits, likes, and dislikes to worry about. And I have lots of experience in staying in other people's apartments, houses, trailers, boats, et cetera whether the owners are there or not. Especially the latter. I am good at finding where they keep the spare light bulbs, the knife sharpener, the garbage bags. Good at making myself at home without disturbing their things and not bad at finding out one hell of a lot about them into the bargain.

How bizarre people are in protecting their privacy from the invited stranger. Some might leave money or personal letters around, yet hide the damnedest things, like paid utility bills for instance. Most of my absent hosts have been considerate in making room in closets and bureau drawers; others made no allowance for my presence in their space, as if to deny the reality of the arrangement. Either way, it's a challenge and usually I do just fine, thanks.

Just from one visit to this place I knew that Nicky Das would leave me lots of room, clean out the bathroom cabinet, dispose of his garbage, change the sheets on the bed, put out fresh towels, and deposit notes on every conceivable question all over the place, with detailed kitchen instructions magnetized to the refrigerator door. And he didn't disappoint me.

I finished my exquisite meal and switched off MacNeil/Lehrer. My interest in the suit/tie and ragtop brigade viewing the world from Washington, D.C. is limited. Their world seldom has much relation to mine or even to anything recognizable in those documentary fragments presented as "background." Maybe those guys have already escaped into outer space. They certainly don't live down here with the rest of us.

The evening stretched out in front of me. I could get a video from the store downstairs and be a couch potato or take the opposite tack and work on my muscle tone at the health club. Neither option held much appeal. When in doubt, I either sleep or read. I wasn't sleepy so I turned to Nicky's bookshelves with anticipation. His taste in subject matter might not be mine, but browsing through a stranger's library can be rewarding. It can lead to some real discoveries, as I knew from past experience.

Vowing to stay open-minded, I went through the shelves, picking out books which looked interesting, flipping through the pages, reading a paragraph here and there, checking out the copyright dates and places.

In no time I had more information about my absent host than I would ever need or want. He was born on August 15, 1947, the day India became independent, and his father had been an officer in the Indian Army during World War II. Nikhil Das himself seems to have spent some time in Britain as well as doing a stint as a police officer in New Delhi.

I am not a fan of war or of stuffy old generals, so Das' library proved dull and too educational for my taste. Finally I picked some light reading, a travel book by a Brit about going down the Ganges, and settled down to enjoy it.

It was almost eleven when the phone rang. It brought me up short. Had to be Alice. No one else knew or cared where I was. I lifted the receiver with some trepidation. The voice was Sam Feng's.

"Miss Keremos ... Helen ... So sorry to bother you. But ... but there is a dead man on the sixteenth floor. Mr. Dennis Gurton. He's dead. I think, I know ... it's murder. Can you come up here ... right away?"

"How? Where?"

"We just found him in Apartment 1605. Lives in Apartment 1607 with his wife Rebecca. They are both lawyers. Mrs. Gurton has been looking for him since she got home from the office this evening. She's been after me to find him, so we looked everywhere. I didn't want to bother you ..."

Nothing brought home the seriousness of the situation as much as Feng's inability to keep his report to the point and totally professional.

"Never mind about that. How did he die, do you know? What makes you think it's murder?"

"I don't know exactly ... but he looks bad, his face is all

swelled up and his neck, it looks broken ... and he's in this empty apartment on the floor. I have to call the police ..."

"I'm coming up. Where are you now?"

"With Mrs. Gurton in their apartment. Number 1607, just across the hall from where we found her husband."

"I am on my way. Now call the cops and his doctor, if he has one. His wife should know."

I hung up, picked up my set of master keys, and made for the elevator. Going up to the sixteenth floor in its immaculate splendour, it occurred to me that with luck life wasn't going to be dull much longer.

▲

IT WAS A TOSS-UP between the body in 1605 and Feng and the widow in 1607. Morbid curiosity won. As I opened the door to 1605, very properly left locked by Feng, the first thing which struck me was the smell of human excrement, which was to be expected in violent death. But also something else which I couldn't place. Perhaps just the odour of an empty, unlived-in apartment.

I had not met Dennis Gurton, so I had to take Feng's word that the body of the young man of thirty or so, dressed in business clothes and laid out in the centre of the empty room, was his. It was on its side in the fetal position, arms and legs tidily together. The shocker was the head. It was twisted unnaturally up to one side, neck broken or at least badly mashed in. Not a pretty sight. Feng's relative incoherence was understandable.

I turned away quickly, swiftly looking around the place just to satisfy myself that the apartment was totally empty, with nobody and nothing around except for the remains of the unfortunate Gurton. There was nothing to see. The place was indeed empty, never been lived in. Without touching anything other than the doorknob, I let myself out silently and crossed the thick carpet to 1607.

Inside was Sam Feng, now in full control of himself, standing as if on guard over a small tear-stained woman. She was under thirty, dressed in expensive office clothes. Clearly, the widow. Under the circumstances it would have been unfair to describe her as "mousy." Unfair but accurate. She lifted her head and looked at me.

"Why!?" she cried. "I don't understand! Why would they kill him? He wasn't doing anything!" A strange thing to say, surely.

I turned to Feng. He shook his head, and reported with evident relief that the police were on their way.

"Mrs. Gurton, Rebecca, I am sorry about your husband ..." What can one say in circumstances like this? Hurriedly, I asked the time-honoured question, "When did you last see him alive?"

"Last night, he came in late, said he had some work to do, I went to bed ... and that's the last time I saw him."

"How about this morning? Didn't you see him over coffee? And what did you mean just now when you said 'why would they kill him?' Who're *they*?"

She looked at me more carefully, wiped her eyes, blew her

nose, sat up straight, and began shedding her "mousiness," which proved to be an illusion.

"I didn't ... I don't know ... Someone must have killed Dennis. That's all I meant."

She paused as if to consider the effect of her answer, then continued changing the focus back to my original question.

"I didn't see him in the morning, so I assumed that he'd left for the office before I got up. He did that sometimes. An early riser. When I got home tonight, he wasn't here. But that's not unusual, so I didn't think anything of it. Then I got worried, he hadn't phoned. I thought perhaps he'd had an accident on his way home. And Dennis is, was, so considerate, we always let each other know when we are held up at the office. So I asked Sam to help me find him ..." She stopped again. All three of us knew she wasn't making too much sense.

"You thought he might have had an accident on the way home? Yet you looked for him in Apartment 1605. Was that on his way home?" I asked hypothetically. "You are a lawyer, aren't you? You should have a better story than that to tell the police."

"I didn't kill him, if that's what you're hinting at and I don't know who did. And who are you to ask me questions, anyway?"

A good point, I thought. Who am I to ask questions? Head of security was a civilian and had no business in a murder investigation, as the cops were sure to point out.

"Just trying to help, that's all. You're husband has been murdered. You will be the prime suspect, you know that. So best pull yourself together before the professionals arrive," I said to be helpful.

Feng looked shocked but the young widow got the message.

"I guess ... well yes, thanks."

As on cue the police arrived. First in dribbles and then in droves. And the place changed from an apartment-house floor into a scene of the crime, just like a made-for-TV movie. I left as soon as I could.

▲

I KNEW IT WOULD BE HIM, although no one had told me. Just intuition or something. Before the office door opened and in walked Detective Staff Sergeant Francis Malory, Homicide Squad, Metropolitan Toronto Police, I was certain he would be the officer in charge. The air was heavy with coincidence; this one was the least of it.

I had sat in that office for two hours, out of the way of the busy boys in blue up on the sixteenth floor, trying to make myself useful doing the few things which I considered to be my responsibility under the circumstances. I needn't have bothered; Feng was there before me every time. He called James Glendenning, the big boss of Diamond; he tried to contact Clare Harwood; he tracked down Wayne Tillion; he got George MacDonald, the maintenance supervisor, out of bed; he answered a thousand questions about the Towers for the police, questions I couldn't have answered anyway. All I ended up doing was making a pot of coffee and a quick call to Alice. And all I got was her answering machine.

Then in walked Malory, followed by a prim young plainclothesman. Fresh and shaved and smiling, sticking out his hand like a long-lost buddy.

"Well, well, Helen Keremos! What a surprise!" he said jovially.

Immediately I knew that he had known since he arrived here that I was head of security, that I was here waiting for him. He had been saving me. My turn to be questioned came only after he knew as much about the crime as I did, and more. Malory liked to appear omniscient. The trick is to ask questions to which you already know the answers. It was characteristic and not unexpected. I was pleased to see him, anyway.

"Ah, Malory. Still haven't graduated to Traffic, I see. Too bad. Nice of you to drop in to see me. Anything I can do for you?"

Malory nodded with appreciation and sat down. Without turning in his direction, he introduced his partner.

"Helen, meet Detective D'Arcy. D'Arcy, Helen Keremos. She and I know each other from the Deerfield case. This is D'Arcy's first assignment in Homicide. You may as well get acquainted. We're all going to see a lot of each other until this thing gets cleared up. Do I smell coffee in that pot?"

Managing to squeeze three cups of tar black liquid out of the coffeepot, I considered Francis Malory and no-first-name D'Arcy.

Signs of change in Malory were subtle. Always a smooth operator, he looked and sounded even smoother, more secure, competent, professional. And — it was totally unfair — time had been good to him. In his forties now, he'd kept much of his hair, while keeping off most of the chin sag. Roused in the middle of the night he'd taken the time to shave and dress with careful casualness. He looked the perfect Ralph Lauren man, down to his tasselled loafers.

Still formatting like a computer disk, I thought D'arcy could turn out to be good backup, a pale imitation or contrast to Malory. His bland face and slight pout did not bode well.

As for the Deerfield case ... well, it could never be just a case to me — considering what Sonia Deerfield and I had meant to each other. Once the "case" part was over, she and I had gone off into the sunset together. We were together for two splendid years up and down the West Coast. Until she decided to settle down in Santa Cruz with a blond alto called Rani, who had tenure at the University of California. How could I compete with that, plus a cabin on the beach? I couldn't and I didn't.

In the Deerfield case I had held a lot of cards and my role had been pretty clear, at least to me. I guess I had given Malory a hard time. In this one I had no cards or status or role. I waited for Malory to rub this in and perhaps to crow a bit. I should've known better.

"Helen, it's going to be a great help to have you here. I know you've just arrived, but tell me what you know and what you think about this messy homicide we have here."

It's against my nature to miss an opening. Since he was going to play nice guy, I slipped in a question.

"What killed him, do you know?"

Without a moment's hesitation he answered, "Officially we won't know until the Medical Examiner tells us, but, unofficially, his windpipe was crushed."

Behind him, D'Arcy stirred uneasily. He didn't like Malory answering my questions. Malory ignored him. I realized then that Malory was showing off his smarts for the benefit of his young colleague. A demonstration exercise, with me as the training dummy. I pressed on.

"That's how he died, but that's not what I asked. What killed him?"

An expert at changing focus, Malory took it in stride.

"We don't know. And it's not the only thing we don't know. Most probably Gurton was killed elsewere, not in the apartment where he was found ... so where was he killed? Why was his body moved? If it was. That's just for starters. Come on, Helen, give. What do you think of Rebecca Gurton? Her story?"

"What is her story? I don't know what she told you. She knows something, for sure more than she told me. But she was genuinely upset. I bet Feng agrees about that and I also bet he repeated what she spilled out when I arrived."

"You tell me."

"Something like 'Why did they kill him? He hadn't done anything!' You mean you still don't know what she meant by that? Why did they go looking for Gurton in an empty apartment? Haven't broken her down yet?"

"About that, well, she claims it was Feng's idea to check Apartment 1605. He doesn't claim anything, except that they had to look 'everywhere.' Who knows what's significant? We do know a lot of other things, but not their significance. Item: Gurton was an environmental lawyer. Could be a lead. Item: he was in debt. Could be a lead. Item: Clare Harwood, the manager, and Nikhil Das, head of security; both left for parts unknown the very night Gurton was iced. Could be a lead. Item: Helen Keremos arrived on the scene at the same time. Coincidence? Well?"

"Environmental lawyer, eh. That smells of politics. No wonder you are being so nice. Don't want to put a foot wrong until you know where the booby traps are. As for coincidence, its no coincidence that I arrived when Harwood and Das left, it's a consequence. All one item. Whether Gurton's death at this time is coincidence ... I take no bets on that. Either way. So what else you got? Time of death? Neighbours?"

"None of the people on that floor admit to knowing or hearing anything last night. So far. As for time, well, unofficially the M.E. figures that Gurton was dead twenty-four hours before he saw the body. So make it about 10 p.m. last night. Give it two hours either side, just to be safe. Here's the interesting part: Harwood and Das are both supposed to have left last night, but no one admits to seeing either of them leave the premises."

"You shitting me? Why Harwood or Das? You got anything against them except that they aren't around? Perhaps it's not a coincidence that Gurton was killed just as they left, perhaps the killer counted on a dumb cop jumping to a conclusion like that. Always the easy way out."

Malory just let it ride but it was too much for D'Arcy. He cleared his throat and spoke:

"Miss Keremos, how did you come to get this job substituting for Mr. Das? Our understanding is that you weren't sent by the head office of Diamond Development Corporation as would normally be the case. Mrs. Harwood hired you directly, is that so? How well do you two know each other?"

Young bull. Malory leaned back and watched me deal with him. I answered:

"Wayne Tillion has been talking, has he? Since one good turn deserves another, you might like to know that Feng considers Tillion some sort of head-office mole, here at Diamond Plaza Towers. Did you ask him how *he* got to be here? What his real job is? "

"We are looking into Tillion. Now answer D'Arcy's questions," Malory cut in magisterially. That was okay by me.

"Clare and I knew each other carnally years ago, currently not at all. As far as I am concerned, Clare Harwood is on vacation with her kids and Nikhil Das is on his way to his sister in India. I took the job to do Clare a favour and because I had nothing better to do in this town. So I sit here and collect my pay while Feng does all the work. I hadn't met Dennis Gurton, and saw Rebecca Gurton for the first time after her husband's death. The only people I have met since I got here are staff — Feng and the security people. And Tillion. But him not even to talk to. I guess it was just hate at first sight. That's it."

"For now. Don't go away too far. There will be lots more."

Malory was still letting me off easy.

"I'll be around. Oh, and just a little thing. Gurton seems to have had an automobile accident very recently. Might be a connection, for what it's worth."

"Good. Thanks." And they walked out, D'Arcy with a piercing look in my direction and Malory still looking calm, rested, and relaxed, although it was almost 3 a.m.

▲

ALICE GOT ME UP in the wee hours by returning my call as
soon as she got back home. I didn't ask her where she'd been
and she didn't volunteer. All we spoke about was the murder.
After I gave her a blow by blow, our conversation continued.

"So your old buddy Malory is just another racist cop,
right? Bet they try to pin it on the East Indian!"

"Cool it, Alice! He isn't my buddy! Just because we
worked together back then doesn't mean I am responsible for
him. And anyway, I don't think he's any more racist than
anyone else. Sure the cops will go after Nick Das, but they will
go after Clare Harwood as well. That's understandable. Neither
of them is around to answer questions and they left just about
when the murder was committed. What do you expect?"

"Yeah, yeah, so you say. But I bet that Harwood woman
comes up smelling of roses and the cops concentrate on the
Indian. Aren't you going to do something about this?"

"About what? Do what?"

"Why, solve the murder, of course! Come on, Helen, don't
be dense. You're a detective, aren't you? This is what you are
good at. I've seen you in action, I know."

It's hard to be bright and cheery at 5:30 in the morning. Especially after getting to bed at three. I didn't feel like arguing with Alice about Malory or Das or racism or my skill as a detective. I felt hassled rather than complimented.

"Alice, it's too early in the morning and too early in the investigation for this. Don't push it, honey, just don't push it. I'll do what I can to make sure no one gets railroaded for this murder, I promise. Not that I think it will be necessary, but I promise. But that's all. And I won't start until after I've had a decent night's sleep. So drop it, okay?"

I didn't hide the irritation in my voice.

There was a moment of silence at the other end of the line.

"You're right, quite right. I'm sorry to have bugged you. Get some rest and call me tomorrow, okay? I miss you, sweetie. Now I wish you hadn't taken this job ..."

"I miss you, too, but if I hadn't taken this job the cops would have the field all to themselves. And you wouldn't have liked that, either. You can't have it both ways."

Then Alice laughed, surprising me as she so often did.

"Oh, Helen, I love you. Good night sweetie, sleep well."

What was that about, what's so funny? I wondered, as I plonked myself back on the pillow. Alice, Alice. I thought of her in the little apartment downtown, sitting on the bed in her black well-darned cotton Danskin — Alice despises spandex — holding on to the phone, perhaps running her other hand through her curly dark hair or rubbing her left knee, which tends to give her trouble and now ... she's naked, her very white skin, much whiter than mine, marked by the seams of the clinging tights, a pinkish line around the edge of her buttocks, disappearing into the crack of her bottom. There are blue veins on the smooth round of her belly and down the inside of her thighs; sweaty moisture in her navel, in the crook of her elbows, and especially under her breasts, tasting salty, I know. The memory of her smell and taste overpower all else as I ride my fist into sleep.

▲

MY WAKE-UP CALL came only three hours later. I wasn't ready for it. After two cups of coffee, I forced myself to shower and dress. I was just shaking the wrinkles out of my best jacket when the phone rang. It was Sam Feng. I wondered whether he'd been to bed at all since the night before.

"Mr. Glendenning is here. He would like to see you, urgently. As soon as you're ready —"

"On my way. Where is he?"

"In the manager's office. Tillion is with him."

Oops! Tillion again. Nice of Feng to warn me. It was barely 9:30, and here was the big boss and the little mole presumably wanting to talk about Gurton's murder. I was down in a flash.

James Glendenning looked me over carefully, taking his time. That was okay by me; I looked him over just as carefully. I had expected a standard-issue baby-boomer businessman and I wasn't far wrong. Maybe he was rather younger and better dressed, with more jewellery and a fancier tie, than I had guessed. He had a long delicate nose on a long horsey face, clear grey eyes, and a meticulously trimmed moustache. He sat forward in Clare's chair, both forearms firmly planted on the empty desktop. Standing at his side, sort of looming over him, was Wayne Tillion, still wearing yesterday's suit, which I now noticed was too tight across the shoulders. He probably worked out, a body builder no less. Tillion, unlike Glendenning, did not look prosperous. But there was one thing they had in common — they both looked scared.

After a moment Glendenning spoke up. He started with the usual throat clearing: "Murder ... terrible, most unfortunate ... innocent people will suffer ... police doing their best, however — " However? Here I started to listen. He was finally about to say something — "responsibility of management to protect our investment. We had to be sure that nothing transpired which could prove detrimental to the future of DP Towers. Since Mr. Gurton had indicated, quite publicly, may I add, that this property was under investigation by his environmental group, well, of course, we had to take the proper precautions. I am sure that Wayne did only what he'd been instructed to do and is in no way involved in Gurton's death. But one has to consider appearances. Wayne's role here at Diamond Plaza Towers, Phase I, could be misinterpreted. By clients, by the media if they get hold of it. The police have already indicated some totally unfounded suspicions regarding Wayne and our corporate interest in Mr. Gurton ... which as I have explained is totally proper and in no way related to his death." Glendenning broke off, looking at me for a reaction.

"What has all that to do with me?" I asked.

"Well, I'm hoping you can help. You work for us now. Clare hired you, with my approval of course, and she has a very high opinion of your skill and experience."

Oh, boy, I thought, if he only knew which of my skills and

41

experience Clare was most high on! Thinking about this made it hard to concentrate on what he was saying.

"Of course, our lawyers are being notified and everyone here is pulling together, I am sure, to get this matter cleared up. However, it has occurred to me that a professional investigator with your background, and already on our payroll, could usefully look into this unfortunate affair. Deal with the police and talk to people here and keep us informed, you understand. And hopefully, establish that this horrible occurrence had nothing to do with the management of Diamond Plaza Towers or any of its employees. Are you with me?"

"If you mean, do I understand, sure I do. You want me to get you and Wayne here out of a tight spot. If you mean, will I do it, that depends."

There was no point beating about the bush. If he didn't like it, too bad. I didn't owe him or DP Towers or Wayne Tillion anything.

"Depends? On what?"

"On answers I get. Like just what did Gurton threaten you with? And what exactly is Wayne's job here? You want me to keep your nuts out of the fire, I have to know just what's involved. Otherwise, it's no go."

It suddenly occurred to me that Glendenning's unexpected faith in my abilities as an investigator had something to do with the fact that Malory and I were old acquaintances. I bet word had gotten around overnight, I bet the police and I were now billed as friends. I didn't intend to disillusion Mr. Glendenning on this point.

"That's reasonable. Well then. Dennis Gurton was legal council for a local Toronto environmental group called Life Watch Ontario. Their symbol is an owl, you've probably seen it on flyers and graffiti. They've been quite active in a number of soil contamination cases, and recently they actually took a property owner to court on behalf of the tenants. And lost, I'm glad to say. LWO badly need to redeem themselves, they need money and a victory of some sort. A high-profile action would give them the necessary publicity and bring out the antidevelopment crazies. You are familiar, I am sure, with just how these groups work. Diamond Plaza Towers is a prime target for people like that. All of us developers are vulnerable. They know that if they go after us publicity is assured. Good publicity for them and bad for us. Once we get bad press we get delays. Antiprogressive lefty politicians and other nuts get into the act and years of planning and preparation, millions of dollars, are at risk. All because of fringe groups like Life Watch."

"Uh, spare me the tearjerker. What about Gurton? What did he have on you?"

"He didn't have anything on us! What happened was his group let it be known that they were investigating a number of properties which were about to be developed for evidence of soil contamination by toxic waste, heavy metals, and such like. If anything like that could be proved about any of them, it would put that property out of the running for years, perhaps forever. One of these properties was the future location of our Phase II. It's right next door; you can see the location from the upper floors. The property was part of the industrial lands north of Highway 401 at Dufferin which the government freed up for housing. We are in the process of purchasing it from the company which acquired it originally. We are committed to development of Phase II, any delay could be fatal ..." He managed to stop himself.

I said, "Fatal, eh. No wonder you're up and going so early today. Slap bang in the middle of a murder case and with a

43

motive the media will love. A public relations nightmare. How about Tillion here? Where does he come in?"

We both looked at Tillion who stared back silently.

"We had to know what Gurton was doing. How this so-called 'investigation' of his was going. I hired Wayne Tillion to keep an eye on Gurton. Wayne has worked for me and my associates before. He's reliable. When the Gurtons moved in here, we put Wayne in as assistant manager to Clare Harwood. So he had reason to be around, access and so forth."

"Better and better! Access — that means keys to all the apartments, among other things. How often did you go through Gurton's briefcase, Wayne? What did you find? And did he find you at it and so you killed him?"

Glendenning moved back hastily in his chair as Tillion plunged across the desk in my direction.

"Enough already!" Tillion almost spat into my face. "I didn't touch that shyster Gurton! Sure, I checked his apartment whenever I could. But you know what? I was invited in! Rebecca really likes me. Wanta make something of it?"

He straightened up, preening. Then turning to Glendenning, he continued, "Why tell her anything? I told you not to worry. The cops have nothing on me."

Glendenning looked a bit spooked. As well he might. You hire a heavy, you'd better be prepared to deal with a heavy. The sex angle was news to him, too. And sex makes a lovely motive and even better tabloid copy. Wayne Tillion was a DP Towers employee hired specifically to spy on Dennis Gurton. What the *Toronto Sun* would make of Wayne's relationship with the grieving widow would put the "soil contamination" problem in the shade. Should this whole story surface, Glendenning and his associates would be out of business in Toronto, at least for a while. And miss out on a heap of profits.

"You may as well know that Wayne has already been telling tales out of school. I don't want to be picky, but last night he put the finger on me to the cops. Who was I? How did I get this job? Like that. Spreading suspicion. Malory wasn't buying it, but just for kicks I repaid the compliment and pointed out that Tillion made an unlikely assistant manager. So expect even more thorough questioning of our Romeo here."

It felt good to be helpful.

Glendenning had to do something quickly, and he didn't have much choice in what that was to be. Wayne was a loose cannon. He had to be prevented from doing any more damage and I was the natural to stop him. I knew too much already, I was there on the spot, I had the experience, I knew the police officer in charge, and presumably I was for sale. Glendenning and I understood all this almost simultaneously.

Who knew what Wayne understood. But what he did was clear enough. He threw down a file folder onto the desk in front of Glendenning and said:

"Here's what I found out about Gurton's investigation of the Phase II property. You'll know better than me just how damaging it is. I'll keep my mouth shut as of now, but remember I have copies of all this stuff and a story to tell if the cops come after me. Jimmy boy, I hope you know what you're doing with this pet female private investigator of yours, but she'd better keep her mouth shut, and out of my way — for all our sakes."

He smiled and strutted dramatically out of the room, his muscular shoulders swinging.

"Well?" I asked Glendenning, reaching casually towards the file folder. Glendenning put his hand on it and shook his head.

"Now, now, Helen. I hope you don't mind me calling you Helen? Good, good. You don't need this information to do your job. Just remember you're working for me."

"Okay, but don't expect to keep anything from me about Gurton and Life Watch, not if you want me to investigate this mess. There is always more than one source for any information. Let's get one thing clear. You want me to keep this matter of Wayne and the Gurtons very, very quiet. Hey, I'm not going to go to the media with it, but Malory has to know, if he doesn't already. What he does with it is up to him. But if you want to talk about damage control, be my guest."

"Damage control. Yes, that's it. What can we do?"

"First off, can you get Clare back here? The cops must be trying to reach her. I would like to talk to her first."

"Clare? What does she have to do with this? But sure, she left her address with my secretary in the office. Let me call and find out."

I waited silently while he punched the phone and got through to his secretary. A minute later I had an address, if you can call it that. It was a box number on a rural route in Muskoka.

"No phone?"

"Guess not."

"Well, that means the cops will find her first. I bet Malory has the Ontario Provincial Police out there by now. Never mind, we'll manage. Get her to cancel her vacation and get back here to work. That will give you an opportunity to 'transfer' Wayne to another position elsewhere without being too obvious. That way he won't be around here making trouble. Cops won't like it but they can't insist that he stay at DP Towers. Of course, they might arrest him but I doubt it. Not unless they have something pretty definitive."

Glendenning watched me.

"I see. What else?"

"Well, somebody killed Gurton. Assuming you didn't and Wayne Tillion didn't, and assuming none of your other minions killed him on your orders, who did? The police will be all over everyone like a swarm of locusts, a number of people innocent or not will be hurt, and a lot of stuff people would rather have hidden will be public property. That's just the way it is, like it or not. So who else is there? That's what I need Clare for. She knows more about the possible cast on the spot. Our best chance is to get a lead quick, shortcutting the investigation. That way it might be possible to save a lot of grief."

Glendenning moved his head impatiently.

"Hell, what d'you think I'm here for this morning? Didn't you hear me? I want this investigation closed as soon as possible and I don't trust the cops not to get sidetracked onto Wayne and our troubles with Life Watch. Anyway, why does it have to be anyone inside? Couldn't the murderer have sneaked in?"

"Don't count on it."

"Well, go work on the case anyway. And keep in touch."

"You got it."

"Good."

He stuck out his hand and we shook.

IN TWENTY-FOUR HOURS at DP Towers I had become transformed from a glorified security guard to a detective on a murder case. Still working for DP Towers Corporation, of course, but in a capacity which felt much better. Thinking of Alice, I grinned to myself. She wanted me on the case in order to protect Nicky Das, whom she'd never met, from being railroaded by the police because he was "a visible minority." And Glendenning wanted me to work on the case because he was afraid the police would dig up something unsavoury about DP Towers and its dealings with Gurton. Nothing would please Alice more than to have Glendenning and his crowd connected with the murder; having Nicky Das as the fall guy would most likely be okay by Glendenning, although he would prefer a non-employee, someone from the outside. And there were probably dozens more crosscurrents out there just waiting for me!

I went up to the sixteenth floor. A uniform gave me an argument but was finally persuaded that I had legitimate business there. Police couldn't keep people out of the whole floor of the building for very long. Apartment 1605, where the body had been found, was still barred to civilians with a yellow scene-of-the-crime tape across the door. I knew it would be out of bounds but had hoped to get to see Rebecca Gurton across the hall in 1607 once again. She turned out not to be home; probably downtown with her lawyer, being taken apart by Malory or D'Arcy.

In lieu of the widow, I decided to check all the neighbouring apartments, starting with 1606. The master list Nicky had given me indicated that, like 1605, it was unoccupied, but once I used my keys to get in I found that, unlike 1605, it wasn't empty at all. It was apparently a model suite, complete with a full set of matched furniture in every room. Police must have checked it, but there was no evidence they had found anything of interest. What I found first of all was a smell. It was in the bedroom and it was the same odour I thought I had detected on Gurton's body the night before. Today I took my time trying to place it. Perfume? grass? cosmetic? cleaner? medicine? herb? — it seemed familiar but I couldn't remember in what context — incense? Incense! Not incense but close! I sat down on the bed and it came to me — the scent of burning candles.

I began a thorough search of what had seemed at first glance an unlived-in, pristine apartment. Knowing they had to be there, I found tiny signs of occupation which had escaped the police. A wax drip on the windowsill. Sticky-sweet ring on the table, smelling of almonds. A bedspread crushed in the middle as well as on the sides, where someone might sit down. These signs figured to be recent since the place had been kept clean and very well dusted. Clare would know of its last legitimate use; when was a potential client last shown through here? One more thing to ask her first chance I got.

Back in the hall, I contemplated my options. Next to 1606

was 1608, registered to a Joyce Dossler. That rang no bells. I knocked. No answer. Moving right along I passed a door marked Service, then an unlabelled locked door. Turning the corner I stopped in front of 1609, trying to recall why the number seemed familiar. Just as it came to me, the door opened and a man who had to be Dr. Melhior Romulu, of the tacky vanity plates, invited me inside, smiling beatifically. He spoke with a barely noticeable accent, unidentifiable at least by me.

"Come in, please. What can I get you? Coffee, perhaps. I expect you haven't had a chance to eat yet this morning. James is so thoughtless. We are just having breakfast, do join us. Eleena!" He knew about my meeting with Glendenning and didn't mind my knowing he knew.

Romulu waved at one of the two women in the room, who came forward and took my hand in both of hers.

"Helen Keremos! I'm so glad to meet you. Heard so much about you. I'm Eleena DeMoulard, and that's Melhior Romulu, as I expect you've already guessed. Do sit down, have some brunch with us. Joyce, this is Helen Keremos, our new head of security. Helen, this is our neighbour, Joyce Dossler."

To say I was overwhelmed would be an understatement. Not just by the unexpected welcome, but more by the place and the people. First of all this was no ordinary condo apartment but two apartments, one of them a corner one, knocked together. The living room was enormous, one whole wall of windows and another of mirrors, making it even grander. It was furnished, well, I guess it was furnished, but the details didn't register for some time. The impression created by the colour scheme was so powerful that I couldn't concentrate. There was nothing extraordinary about the colours themselves, only about the way they were used. They ran from white to pale beige, virtually monochromatic. Hard to describe the overall effect; a melting, a running together, shapelessness. Floor, rugs, walls, ceiling, tables, chairs, sofas, pictures — no contrast, no edges. Facing southeast, the air was thick with brilliant light. Walking through it was like wading through reflections. Like being in a desert underwater.

Two brightly coloured objects, mirrored in the walls, stood out from the seeming monotony. One was probably an enormous vase, it was hard to tell exactly. About five feet tall, oval like an elongated egg, it was blue. An electric blue, the kind met only in dreams or on the fins of tropical fish. The other was a nubby wall hanging, a rough-textured tapestry in brilliant coral. These two startling splashes of colour, far from detracting from the effect of white-on-beige, only emphasized the amazing aquarium-like quality of the place.

Both inhabitants were fitted perfectly into this marvellous stage. Eleena DeMoulard was a fascinating beauty, whatever her real name. A Madonna with flaxen hair flowing down her shoulders, long smooth brown limbs beautifully displayed in an off-white lounging suit of silk or some similar material, rich and soft. She wore no jewellery, and if there was makeup on her face, it wasn't apparent to me. I thought her eyes would be blue but, no, they were light brown, or yellow or gold or whatever. Devastating. On top of all this was the way she moved. Not languid and mannered as could have been expected, but vital and lively like a young colt.

I couldn't think of anyone who looked less like a regular dentist than Doctor Melhior Romulu. He was very tall and very thin, almost emaciated, with large feet and hands with knobby knuckles. I couldn't imagine them in anybody's mouth. His sandy hair was combed back and plastered down like a caricature from the thirties. A wispy moustache clung to his face over full fleshy lips and straight, yellowing teeth. However, the lower part of his face went unnoticed because the feature which drew all eyes were the enormous shelflike eyebrows. Like Stalin's. One straight, bushy, black rug hanging over a pair of small, twinkly, coal-black eyes! It was as if his face was put together from three modules, each from a different man — at the top hair, forehead, next eyebrows and eyes, then everything from the nose down to the pointy chin.

Making the most of this bizarre face and body was a fitted suit of extravagant cut in what looked like linen in brown-on-beige vertical stripes. He had espadrilles on bare feet, tieless white shirt buttoned to the top, a large signet ring on his right hand, and a wide gold band on the wedding finger.

It had taken me a moment or two to take all this in, and by then we women were sitting on wicker chairs around a wicker table laden with beige ironstone ware. On my left, swinging doors led to the unseen kitchen, into which Romulu promptly disappeared. I figured we were being entertained in the breakfast area and there was a formal dining room hidden somewhere on the other side, in what would have been the other apartment.

As Eleena poured coffee, I finally became aware of the third person in the room: Joyce Dossler. I vaguely remembered Feng mentioning her in connection with the two teenaged boys we saw in the lobby the previous night. One of them was her son, Norman. It seemed a long time ago.

Joyce Dossler sat across the table and stared at me with naive interest. A faded woman in her early forties, she looked totally out of place in this extravagant décor. She wore the hairdo, makeup, and leisure clothes appropriate for brunch in a suburban family room. And this most definitely did not qualify.

Fresh brioches and croissants were handed round, together

with butter, honey and marmalade, apple juice, and sliced melon. Soon Melhior appeared with omelettes. Our hosts' taste in breakfasts didn't run to anything out of the ordinary, I noticed gratefully. But no strawberry jam or blueberries, either. Colour coordination taken to such considerable lengths was easy enough at breakfast. Wonder what they would serve for dinner, I thought. Perhaps the colour scheme in the proper dining room was different.

Melhior Romulu, very much the gracious host, tried for a while to keep the conversation to platitudes. He was very good at them himself, knew it and consciously enjoyed playing his part. Joyce Dossler, totally unaware, broke the polished surface of his chitchat by turning to me with a question:

"Miss Keremos, oh, do tell about the murder! You must know so much *more* about it than we do, do tell us! Are the police really going to arrest Rebecca? It's always the spouse who's suspected first, isn't it? That's what my Richard always said."

It was highly doubtful that I knew more than these three people knew about the murder, but I knew different things. Things Melhior and Eleena also wanted to know.

"I don't know very much, although I saw the body. As for any arrests, sorry, but the police don't confide in me. But yes, a spouse is the natural suspect. Do you believe Mrs. Gurton killed her husband?" I answered politely.

"Yes, tell us what you think, Joyce. You knew the Gurtons better than any of us, didn't you? What kind of man was Gurton? What kind of a marriage did they have?" jumped in Romulu. I had the feeling he had his own opinion about the Gurtons and their marriage and was drawing out Dossler's. For my benefit?

"Oh, dear, I don't know. They seemed a perfectly nice

couple. We had them over to a party once, before poor Richard passed away, and we both liked them. Richard was my husband, you know, I'm a widow now. Anyway he thought they were both pretty smart lawyers. And Richard knew about things like that. I remember he said that it was a pity Dennis Gurton worked for that funny environmental group, he would never make any money that way. As it was, it was Rebecca who was making the money in the family. Richard didn't think that was a good idea. For the woman to be making more than her husband, I mean. Richard believed in traditional values."

Dossler went back to her omelette, sparing us more of "poor Richard's" opinions at least for the time being.

"Why, that must have been before you moved in here, Joyce! What a coincidence that you bought an apartment right next to theirs!" commented Romulu.

"Oh, not at all. I bought in here first, they moved in later. I thought you knew that, Mel." Dossler said, obviously surprised.

Romulu did know. His artless comment was for my benefit. Anyway, it was quite a coincidence, whoever had followed whom.

"Well, Dennis always struck me as a very committed person. I didn't know him that well, but he really seemed to believe in what LWO was doing. It wasn't just a job for him. Didn't you think so, Melhior?" Eleena took the conversational ball.

"Since you ask, I would say that Dennis Gurton wanted two things more than anything in the world. One of them was to save life on earth," Romulu declared, and then stopped dramatically.

"And the other?" asked Joyce Dossler predictably.

"And the other was to own a monster house with all the trimmings!"

"You're joking, Mel! How can you be so cynical. Dennis wasn't a hypocrite about the environment. Helen, don't listen to him."

"I didn't say he was a hypocrite. Like many perfectly genuine people, he wanted to have his cake and eat it, too. He wanted to do good and live well at the same time. To save the world without giving up any of its comforts and privileges."

"Is that why he was killed, in your opinion, Dr. Romulu?" I asked.

"Definitely, yes. Call me Mel."

▲

I WENT BACK TO MY APARTMENT with plenty to think about. Everything I had heard so far this day made me want to talk to Rebecca Gurton. I wondered how Malory was getting on with her and when he would get after me again. Of course he was busy. Some cases leave you scrambling for leads; this case was crawling with them, an embarrassment of leads. He and his boys would have to chase down each and every one. Not me, I couldn't and wouldn't. Neither could I afford to miss anything. Which left me in a dilemma.

There were things I had learned over the course of the morning from Glendenning, Tillion, Dossler, and Romulu which Malory probably didn't know. And he had all the medical and routine police stuff — who, when, last seen, examination of the body, apartments, office — plus whatever he'd gotten from personal interrogation of Rebecca Gurton, the staff, the neighbours, and by now possibly Clare Harwood, which might be news to me. If an informal exchange of information could be arranged, both of us would be better off and I wouldn't have to worry about all the leads I couldn't follow. The question was, would he see it this way?

Of course that funny smell I picked up near the body, which seemed to match the candle scent in the model suite, and the evidence of occupation I found there would remain my little secret. He would have his little secrets also, that was for sure. Still, it was worth a try.

In the apartment I listened to the phone messages. Feng with a routine report. He wanted me to know that everything was under control, he was only going home to change and would be back on duty by 3 p.m. Good for him. Next was Malory looking for me. He had to see me a.s.a.p. That was nice. Then Alice. She just wanted me to call. Well, I wanted to see her. Since Feng was being so all-fired keen, I reckoned I wouldn't be missed if I played hookey and stayed downtown for the night. I called back and told her machine to expect me.

So what next? I thought I'd better pretend to be working at my security job for a while. On the way to the office, over just two floors and a few hundred metres of maroon carpet, I was accosted no less than six times by residents who wanted to be told more about the murder. They had somehow found out who I was, or rather whom I was replacing. Some of these good solid Canadians, who I am sure had never spoken to Das —

except possibly to complain — and certainly not to each other, were talking away a blue streak in elevators and corridors. There's nothing like a local murder to break the ice, I thought.

Finally I made it to the peace and safety of the security office, hoping to be able to put my feet up and have a private think. Instead I found a six-page, single-spaced memo on my desk, from Feng. He was reporting on his interrogations by the police, questions and answers, every word. He believed in the chain of command. With a groan I sat down and read it. More input, lots of it.

What I learned was mostly negatives but no less important for that. Cops wanted to pin down everyone's movements on the night Gurton died. They were especially interested in Das and Harwood and wanted to find them as quickly as possible. They also wanted any gossip about the relationships between the residents of the sixteenth floor, but Feng couldn't help them there very much. To him these people were just names, faces, and apartment numbers. Their movements that night were another matter. Feng gave the cops all he knew and could find out, not omitting anything he had on Wayne Tillion and that was quite a bit. A guy not to be taken lightly.

The investigation was hampered by a timetable which had to cover all eventualities, since the time of death couldn't be established with any exactness. From Feng's account I surmised that the security staff on duty that night, which included Selena Amos and Feng himself, alibied each other for the whole period over which the murder could have been committed. Nobody else had an alibi of any sort. Not even Romulu and DeMoulard could alibi each other, since they came home separately, well within the time span in which the murder took place. There was no one to give Rebecca Gurton an alibi and Joyce Dossler had been home alone a good part of

57

the time, until her son Norman showed up. Feng didn't know where Tillion had been; he wasn't seen all evening.

Many of the questions concerned the possibility of unauthorized access. How could an outsider get in or a resident come and go without being spotted by security? There is no such thing as a building which cannot be entered or security which cannot be bypassed. Cops know that. What they wanted from Feng was his opinion on who could do so and how. But no matter how much pressure they put on him, it appeared from his own account that Feng wouldn't oblige them. He was loyalty and professionalism personified. Diamond Plaza Towers was covered by the best security system money could buy. It was especially secure when he, Feng, was on duty. Residents could perhaps have slipped in and out without being noted specifically, but no outsider had gotten past him that night, he was sure. Too bad that all this loyalty wouldn't endear Sam Feng to his boss, James Glendenning. Feng was making it just that much more difficult for Glendenning to claim someone unconnected with DP Towers as the culprit.

I finished Feng's report and was considering deserting my post when the phone rang.

"Hello, Helen, it's Clare. Helen, you've got to help me, *please*. I've got to talk to you."

"Sure, Clare, now take it easy. Where are you? Can you talk?"

"That's just the problem. I'm downtown at police headquarters. They picked me up at the cottage and brought me directly here. So I can't talk now and I don't know how long it's going to be. But I must see you as soon as possible."

" You sure it's me you need and not a lawyer, Clare? What kind of trouble are you in?"

"Damn it, Helen, just listen to me! I don't want a lawyer! I didn't kill Dennis Gurton. But I need to talk to you."

"Okay, okay. Keep your cool. I will be staying at the downtown apartment tonight with Alice. Call me there as soon as you can. I'll pick you up and we'll talk. Okay?"

She hung up in my ear, perhaps because someone was there or perhaps in exasperation. There was no way of knowing. Anyhow, Clare now knew how to reach me later, assuming she still wanted to talk.

▲

FOLLOW ME ANYWHERE and I'll blow in your ear ... Yes ... What's this little mark on the back of your neck? Been necking with a ... You've got the greatest ass in the Western Hemisphere, did you know that? Yes, you did, I've told you that before ... How about moving your leg ... the other leg, not this one! What are you, an octopus? ... Let's take a break. I'm out of breath ... This is no time to worry about the mattress slipping off the bed ..."

"Don't start anything you don't mean to finish ... Ahaaah!"

Sounds, words, noises, sighs, kissing and hissing, slurping and grinding, farts and slaps, orgasmic cries ...

After a while we got hungry and Alice volunteered to get some food together. We were into the second bottle of wine, the mattress was back on the bed, and I lay on it watching her manoeuvre in the kitchen, barefoot and bare-assed. There are advantages to a one-room apartment.

Alice has deep grey eyes and dark curly hair, which springs up over her forehead like a mane. Her pubic hair is unusually straight and silky, like the hair on her legs. I wonder at her legs, well-defined muscles stretch and bunch in perfect harmony. She is shorter than I am by about five inches, her body so well proportioned she seems even smaller. Next to Alice I'm an awkward string bean, full of bony angles and lined flesh.

This had been our best lovemaking in weeks. There was no point commenting on it, we both knew it and understood why. It goes against current revealed wisdom but sometimes it's better not to analyse a relationship too closely. Living things are known to shrivel up and die under a microscope. We were doing okay again and that's all that mattered.

Sitting on the bed we ate the refrigerator leftovers with our fingers, feeding each other, smacking our lips, making rude monkey noises, and laughing. Even the cold, day-old Chinese take-out tasted great.

Alice belched loudly, collapsed full-length on the bed, and said, "Enough of this orgy. Now pay for your supper. Tell me all. I've got the outline, now I want more."

"Insatiable as usual, eh. Okay, here goes. To start with, you'll be pleased to know that I'm now working on this murder case for Mr. James Glendenning of Diamond Plaza Towers Corporation. It's my job to find 'whodunit,' as long as it's not Mr. Glendenning or Wayne Tillion, and preferably not any other employee of the company. Now isn't that good news?"

"You're putting me on! You cannot work for these people."

"But I already work for them. Who d'you think signs my

cheques as head of security? So what's the difference? My, my, I thought you would be pleased. I can save Nikhil Das from the nasty cops all in the line of duty."

"Sometimes I despair for you, Helen. You know damn well what I mean. Now get on with it."

"You're no fun. Hey, I take that back! Not to worry about Glendenning and Tillion getting off scot-free. Cops have had an earful about Tillion and will hang him out to dry, whatever Glendenning says. I figure that area will be well covered by the cops and I can concentrate on others."

"What area?"

"I mean Dennis Gurton's work for Life Watch, you know all that environmental business. Phase II property and DP Towers and Corporation. It's right down the cops' alley and I couldn't get near it. Let them do the digging."

"I hope you're right."

"Trust me."

"What are you going to concentrate on then?"

"Look what I have to go on. First, that model suite. You want to know what I think? I think Gurton was in that bedroom before he died! Maybe he was killed there, then the body moved to the empty apartment next door."

"Why move the body? Wouldn't that be dangerous?"

"Sure, there would be danger of being seen with the body between apartments, but the killer must have figured it was even more dangerous to leave it there. So the location must point to the killer somehow. You see, that model suite with the nice bed and all looks very inviting for clandestine meetings of a certain sort," I said leering at Alice and she grinned back.

"Keep your mind on business. You mean it was a love nest, 'a randyvoo!' Oh, I like that, at last some sex in that dreary place. But who, with whom?"

61

Alice was having a good time, playing with words, enjoying the puzzle, the hunt for answers. She pulled the covers over her body and settled down again, propped up on her elbow. I sat on the edge of the bed, still cooling off.

"Yes, finally some 'illicit sex' — how d'you like that? But 'the who with whom' is tricky. Presumably Dennis Gurton met someone in that apartment. We don't know who and we don't know why. But let's assume for sex, and let's assume it wasn't the first time. His lover would then be a prime suspect. Which is why his body would be moved into a neutral space like that empty apartment.

"We don't know anything about Dennis Gurton. So his lover could be anyone, male or female. It's a wide-open field at the moment. Then again, maybe it wasn't a lover, maybe he met someone in that apartment for some reason connected to the Phase II property investigation. If that was the case, why move the body?"

"Either way, it had to be someone on the premises, right? Someone who lives in DP Towers."

"Or works."

"Right, or works. So who's your pick?"

"None as yet. Anyway the Great Detective can't reveal all she knows or she couldn't dazzle you with her insight. Seriously, who worries me is Clare."

"Clare! You think Clare and Gurton ... You think maybe she killed him, is that it?"

"I don't think, but who knows? Her phone call to me does suggest that she's involved in some way. Otherwise, why the panic?"

"Well, you know her, I don't. Is it likely Gurton would be her lover?"

"I have no idea. I don't know anything about her private

life currently. It's possible, I guess. But, of course, there are other possibilities."

"Like what? Involving Clare?"

"Well, for one thing, she and Gurton could be meeting for reasons other than sexual. For instance, perhaps she was helping him with information about plans for Phase II. That means she was working against her employer, so she would want to keep it quiet."

"But you said it was sex! Don't disapoint me now."

"I still think the place reeked of sex. After all, for a business meeting, why the candles? There are still other possibilities. Perhaps Gurton saw someone like his wife, for instance, going into that apartment and followed. Perhaps he was killed because he caught someone at it."

"You believe this Wayne Tillion was making it with Rebecca Gurton? If Wayne and Rebecca disposed of Dennis, why would Wayne boast about their relationship? Is he dumb enough not to see the danger? And how does Clare come into this?"

How was I to know? I sighed.

"Sweetie, you know I don't know the answers. All we can do here is sort out the most useful questions. Wayne Tillion, Rebecca Gurton, and Clare Harwood are all question marks. But there are others. Remember that trio in Apartment 1609 I told you about?"

"Wait, I remember those names Melhior Romulu, Elaina Demustard, and Joyce Somebody ... "

"That's Eleena DeMoulard and Joyce Dossler."

"Yeah, yeah. What a bizarre scene that must have been. I wish I could meet these people. Not exactly what you'd expect to find in a suburban high rise. You have all the luck. But tell me, is that a ménage à trois or what?"

"You know, that never occurred to me! Joyce Dossler doesn't seem to fit with the other two at all. A not-too-bright, middle-class, out-of-her-depth recent widow is how she struck me. But that might just be an added fillip for the likes of Mel and Eleena. Or it might be an illusion, anyway. But what made you think of them as a threesome?"

"You should study the personal columns. Try *NOW* weekly, for instance. It would open your eyes to a lot of things. But it's not likely in this case, is it?"

"It didn't strike me that way at the time, no. I guess I've led a sheltered life. And I see that I'd better spend more time improving my mind with uplifting literature, like you! Listen, what interested me most is that comment of Romulu's about Gurton wanting to have his cake and eat it, too. I told you about that. What do you think?"

"What's so strange about that? That's what everyone wants. It's what we are about, isn't it? Except you, of course. And this guy, Melhior. You and he must have a lot in common. Sometimes you're so sweet and old-fashioned, Helen."

"So that's why you laugh at me when I point out that you can't have it both ways, eh? Well, I'll be damned!"

"I wouldn't have you any other way, love."

"Good, because I'm not about to change. Is this a generation gap, or what? Instruct me."

"Could be. So how old is Romulu, anyway? You never said."

"About my age, I guess. So you could be right. My, my. It's not that we wouldn't like to have it both ways, you know, it's that in our experience it doesn't happen. Maybe that's where the age difference comes in. To get back to our point here, I don't think Mel Romulu was talking in generalities about Gurton wanting 'to do good and do well.' He said something quite specific about a 'monster home.' Now, even you will admit there might be some conflict between being a committed environmentalist and wanting a monster home and all. Surely somewhere along the line you can only 'do well' at the expense of 'doing good?' Or vice versa, I guess. Either way then, you have to choose. Not so, Pollyanna?"

"I won't argue. Let's just take it that Gurton was after money and would sell out if he had the opportunity. Or had already sold out. How would Romulu know about any of that?"

"He sure knows more than he's telling. It all comes back to what kind of guy Gurton was. Romulu seems to have a bead on Gurton. Plus I bet he knows quite a bit of what goes on at the Towers in general."

"How about this Romulu, he's filthy rich, isn't he?"

"Probably. So?"

"So, I would want to know more about him, too. Don't forget him and his lovely lady, this Eleena."

"No chance."

"Helen! Enough already. Come over here and let's rock 'n' roll a bit more."

We didn't last long. The wine took its toll and soon after we were asleep in a tangle of arms and legs. Cradling Alice's sleeping body in my arms, the last thing I recalled thinking is that Clare hadn't phoned.

▲

I CAN'T REMEMBER the last time I'd gotten as mad as I did when I returned to my apartment in the Towers next morning and found it being torn up. Four cops were going meticiously through every bit of Nikhil Das' stuff, every piece of paper, every book, every jar in the kitchen. D'Arcy was in charge and Malory was nowhere to be seen when I walked in on them and blew my stack.

"What the hell d'you think you're doing! You've no business here. This is my place now. I don't recall giving permission for this search."

"Sorry about that, Miss Keremos," said D'Arcy, not looking sorry at all. "We couldn't find you last night and no one knew when you would be back. We couldn't wait forever, you know, so we decided to go ahead this morning, anyway."

"Wait for ever? Why do you want to search this place at all? Is every apartment in the whole building getting this treatment?"

"No, of course not. Now, Miss Keremos, there is no need to be so upset, your things have been set aside, we didn't touch them."

66

"Nice of you! But that doesn't answer my question. What's your authority for going through Mr. Das' apartment while he's away? Did you get his permission?"

I was getting a bad feeling about this. Something was wrong, I could tell by the way D'Arcy smiled at me, like the proverbial cat with the canary.

"We have information which leads us to believe that Mr. Das may be involved in the murder of Mr. Gurton. That's all the authority we need."

Don't you just love bureaucratic language? Everything so carefully qualified that nothing can be pinned down.

"Where's Malory?" I didn't want to talk to this clown D'Arcy any more in case I did something I might regret. Like spit in his eye. He stood in the living-room doorway, towering over me by a good six inches. I heard one of the cops snigger behind him. He was playing to an audience.

"Sergeant Malory is in conference downstairs. I'll let him know you were asking for him."

"Don't put yourself out. I'll find him. And I want you, all of you, out of here by the time I get back."

"Or else?" D'Arcy added sarcastically, raising an eyebrow. But I didn't wait.

In the elevator again, I wondered, not for the first time, how it was that the Toronto police force would hold and promote a horse's ass the likes of D'Arcy as well as good, smart cops like Malory. Do the powers-that-be see this as part of their noble effort to have the police reflect the community? Isn't it bad enough to have a police force made up mainly of large white males? Do so many of them have to be stupid as well?

To be halfway fair, I knew that D'Arcy was more of a problem for Malory than he could ever be for me or any other citizen. It goes without saying that good cops hate the other kind more than we can imagine. But in the long run it is the misplaced police solidarity of the good guys which keeps the force safe for bad apples.

My internal diatribe on the cops had come full circle, as it always did. There was no getting away from death, taxes, and the dumb minions of institutions. Pointless to get in a sweat about it, I always told myself, and always got fiercely mad, anyway.

I hoped that seeing and talking to Malory would make me feel better and at least clear up the matter of Nicky Das. In this case, hope being the mother of fools.

Malory was in the security office, at *my* desk, not in any conference but on the phone. He hung up as I stomped in, got up, and propped himself on the edge of the desk, thereby letting me have the chair. This morning he was impressive in his well-cut three-piece suit, tasteful tie, blow-dried hair.

Malory would never be crudely obnoxious like D'Arcy. His were police tactics with class. He knew why I was angry and tried to be pleasant, letting me cool down. But he started out making things worse.

"Sorry about that, Helen. Couldn't be helped, you know. I did try to find you last night to let you know we had to toss that apartment. The boys will be through up there momentarily, they will leave everything nice and tidy, I promise. Actually, I don't think they've found anything incriminating as yet —"

"Malory, what is going on? Will you stop blathering and tell me why you decided to go after Das like this?"

"Oh, didn't D'Arcy tell you? Das never left for India. We checked at the airport."

"No, D'Arcy never told me, as you well know! Anyway so what! Maybe Das didn't fly direct. Maybe he went via New

68

York, maybe a friend drove him to Buffalo. There are a million reasons why you couldn't find his name on a flight to India."

"Oh, but we did! He was booked on Air Canada three weeks ago. All paid for and everything. He certainly meant to go. But he didn't make the flight ... Now d'you understand why we are interested in Mr. Das?"

I was silent, considering. Malory was right. That did change things. There were objective grounds for the police to put Das high on their list of suspects. It was harder for me. After all, I had sipped malt whisky with him just a few hours before the murder. I had to imagine Das seeing me off the premises and, then, sneaking out and breaking Gurton's windpipe! In between packing and preparing the apartment for my occupancy, all of which must have taken hours.

It wasn't impossible, but subjectively it was damn improbable.

There were other questions. I threw them at Malory.

"If Das killed Gurton, why not go to India as planned? Best thing to do, surely."

"It's a puzzle, I don't deny it. I don't have an opinion on Das. We don't even know when he left the building or how. Checking the cab companies now. By the way, what did you think of him? Tell me, it might help."

"Well, if you looked around his apartment, you have some idea. Very much an immigrant still, I would say. You know, we always assume immigrants to Canada are poor or otherwise unfortunate and come here to escape or to come up in the world. But there are other reasons for immigrating. It seemed to me that Das had come down in the world in coming to Canada. From his bookshelves and conversation I would say he is an upper-class, educated Anglophile and probably pretty conflicted about it. Difficult for an Indian patriot, I would imagine. If you can find anything in that as a reason for Das to kill Dennis Gurton, well, I don't see it."

Malory shifted from one buttock to the other, not too subtly letting me know he was bored. He had expected something more substantial.

"Maybe not yet, but give us time. Anyway, so maybe he personally didn't ice Gurton. Doesn't mean he's not involved in some way we know nothing about. All I can see is that he was here at the pertinent time, he's not here now, and he didn't go where he claimed to be going. That makes him a suspect. Well?"

"You must have a ton of suspects if that's all it takes."

Malory shrugged. I decided to change the subject and lower the temperature of our conversation.

"Who all else is on your list? How about Tillion, d'you like him?" I asked Malory.

"He's a good one, that Tillion. He's got a previous: assault with a deadly weapon, suspended. I guess you know he was spying on Gurton for Glendenning and making out with Gurton's wife, from all accounts, including his own. She doesn't deny it, by the way. Definitely he's a suspect and if I had a shred of evidence that he was around on the sixteenth floor night before last, I would have the cuffs on him. But I don't."

"A previous for assault, opportunity, and possible motive, and that's not enough? What d'you want, an eyewitness?"

"I told you and you damn well know that I have to place him on the scene at the time of the crime! You would be the first to tell me that I haven't got bubbkes if it was somebody you were going to bat for."

He had a point. But so did I.

"Yeah, and vice versa. If Tillion didn't have Glendenning at his back, would you be quite so careful?"

"Maybe not, but that's just common sense. I would love to land Tillion, and his boss, for that matter, but it won't help if I show my hand before I have the cards."

"So what else is in your hand? What about the widow? She tell you anything useful?"

"Depends what you mean by useful. This Rebecca Gurton is quite something. A hot-shot lawyer, it turns out. Just what I need. She did put me on to Glendenning and the Life Watch matter. She says that is what you and Feng heard her refer to just after the body was found. She says! She also insists that she doesn't know the details of her husband's investigation or what, if anything, he'd found out which would threaten Diamond Plaza Towers. She claims not to know about Tillion's job. Personally, I don't buy it. We're digging, you bet. It's early days. You got anything else for me?"

"Not much. Let's see ... Joyce Dossler knew the Gurtons before she moved here. Dr. Melhior Romulu seems to know more about Dennis Gurton than might be expected, given they haven't been neighbours all that long. And they all live on the sixteenth floor and, as you know, nobody there has an alibi."

"Oh? Interesting. Anything else?"

"Nothing solid. But tell me, how was Dennis Gurton killed? D'you know yet?"

"Damn it, no. Broken windpipe, as you know, but how it was done, the sawbones cannot tell me. A blow from something, maybe a karate kick, even the edge of the hand is a possibility." Suddenly he grinned, " Would it be sexist to say that it's not likely the perpetrator is a woman?"

"It's sexist to jump to conclusions about what either men

or women can and cannot do. And you're talking skill here. Anyone can learn karate."

"Hey, I just said 'not likely,' make that less likely, than a full-grown man. For example, I would pick Tillion over any of the women involved so far. Wouldn't you?"

Malory looked at me quizzically, having his fun. He was up to something.

"Who are the women involved so far. Let's see: Rebecca Gurton, for sure, Joyce Dossler, maybe, Eleena DeMoulard ... Who else?"

We were both being disingenuous, but that was the name of the game.

"Well, there is Clare Harwood," Malory said with an uncharacteristic casualness, "one female you haven't mentioned."

"Oh? Should I have? What about Clare? How is she involved?"

"I was hoping you would tell me! Don't hold out on me, Helen. I know you are loyalty personified, but she is a suspect and she called you from downtown last night. What did she tell you?"

He'd dropped the pose and became pressing.

"Nothing. Why is she a suspect?"

We were barking at each other now; D'Arcy would have loved it.

"Nothing! Come on, Helen! She's in a state. I saw her, so I know she was scared. She calls you and doesn't say anything? Don't kid a kidder."

"She said she would call back later. But she didn't. And where is she now? And again, what makes her a suspect? You want my cooperation, tell me that at least."

"My pleasure. She was seen coming down from the sixteenth floor around eleven the night of the murder. That good enough for you?"

"Seen by whom? Where?"

"By George MacDonald, the super. He'd been working late, moonlighting I bet, for one of the tenants on the ninth floor. We checked, so don't get your hopes up. He was on his way home, waiting for an elevator to go down to the lobby. On the board he saw one elevator on its way down from the penthouse, then it stopped at the sixteenth floor just long enough to let someone get on and then came right down to where he was, on the ninth floor. The doors opened, there was Clare Harwood, whom he believed had left for vacation earlier that evening. Naturally he was surprised but didn't comment. She got off on the second floor. He went down to the lobby and out to his car in the employee parking lot. Security confirms this. They set the time at between ten and eleven."

"Security could have only confirmed that MacDonald left the building. They didn't see Clare, did they?" I said, remembering Feng's report which didn't mention Clare. "So all you have is his say-so. What kind of a guy is he?"

"A Brit, working stiff, bit over the hill. Give me a reason why he would lie about this."

"She's his boss, maybe he doesn't like her. Anyway, how could he tell she'd gotten on the elevator on the sixteenth floor? Maybe she was already on it and someone else got off on the sixteenth."

I was grasping at straws and I knew it. Anyway, I wished I had met this George MacDonald, but as it was I didn't even remember seeing him. "Helen, you're too smart to take that line. Clare Harwood admitted being on the sixteenth floor that night! She claims to have gone up to check the model suite, that's 1606, before leaving for her vacation. Very conscientious of her, eh? Gurton's body was found in Suite 1605, remember?"

He fell silent, looking at me.

First Nicky Das and now Clare Harwood. Nothing but bad news and I couldn't even tell if Malory was gloating, if he had any more up his sleeve. For a fleeting moment I wondered what I'd tell Alice.

"So you don't believe her, about the model suite, I mean?" I asked tentatively. He rolled his eyes, not bothering to answer.

"What else you got?" I continued, feeling a little better.

"Isn't that enough? I've got a plate-full of suspects, unexplained circumstances, lies, and evasions. What more could I ask for?"

Malory had his own troubles, I was glad to see.

"You've had more time to think about this; what connection can there be between Gurton and these two? I mean Das and Harwood. Together or separately?"

"That's what I mean to find out. Which is why D'Arcy is after every scrap of information on Das until we find him, if it takes all year. And I'm gonna shake Harwood loose from her fillings if I have to. And you are going to help us."

It wasn't a question.

"What d'you want from me? Hell, I just got here. What can I get that your boys cannot?"

"Speak sweetly to Clare Harwood. She's scared plenty already and I'll be after her; she is bound to come to you, to ask for your help, like she did last night."

Malory was deadly serious. He really expected me to be his snitch. I must have showed my outrage because he continued without a break.

"And don't come over all scruples and female solidarity at me. I don't have any time for that nonsense. Think of it this way: Nihil Das remains our prime suspect and D'Arcy will be on his case, day and night. Does that make you feel any better?"

He got off the desk, gave me a cool stare, and moved to the door. As he opened it, he turned and said, "Call me when you get anything out of Harwood. I'll be waiting."

▲

I'D HAD A JOB DONE ON ME. Malory had set me up. I went over what had, after all, been a pretty commonplace conversation and had to admit that his had been a masterly performance. I wasn't concerned about the problem he'd tried to set up for me — the choice between selling out Clare Harwood or throwing Nick Das to the wolves. I can tell a phony ethical dilemma when it hits me in the eye and could cope with that okay. What worried me was that I hadn't seen it coming, that I wasn't able to turn the tables. Proving that I wasn't as sharp as I like to think I am. My edge just wasn't there.

The hell with pretending to be on security. I made a beeline for the manager's office, hoping to catch Clare. She was there, on the phone. Looking up when I entered, she waved me out again, mouthing "later," her hand over the mouthpiece. So after all that panic last night, she didn't want to see me! Hell with "later." No way was I going to hang around feeling as I did. What I needed was a walk, I decided. To clear my mind, steady my nerves, stretch my muscles. Make me feel more like my old self again.

In the lobby Wayne Tillion walked past me, carrying a sports bag, on his way to the health club. He ignored me. He wore a tank top with a towel over his shoulder. Why is it that men who bulge out of tank tops believe they look good because of their muscles, whether it's true or not? While when women bulge, they assume it's fat and ugly, whether it's true or not? Now there's a question for research!

I asked Feng, back on duty, what Tillion was doing there. I'd hoped Glendenning had gotten rid of him.

"He's on his day off, I believe." In Feng's tone was the implication that it was hard to distinguish between Tillion's days off and days on. I shrugged and asked about George MacDonald. Feng seemed mildly surprised.

"Yes, I mentioned him in my report. Night of murder he'd left building late. George often does private work after hours. That's okay by management. Keeps residents happy. No problem."

"What kind of a man is George MacDonald?" I asked. Feng opened his eyes wide. It wasn't the kind of question he was used to answering.

"Kind of man? He's experienced supervisor. No problem." Feng sounded uncomfortable, his usually perfectly idiomatic English getting wobbly.

"You don't like him?" That wasn't really a proper question, so I tried again, "How d'you get on with him?"

"Fine, fine. No problem. Only ..." Here Feng dropped his voice, looked away, and said, "Only he don't like Asian people. He was in Burma during World War. Prisoner of war of the Japanese. Had very, very bad time. Very proud man ... Nothing to do with me, yes?"

"Nothing at all, I see. How does he get along with Mrs. Harwood?" I asked. Both Feng and I were relieved to have the subject changed. Scars from forty-five years ago! Christ! As if we didn't have enough problems.

"Oh, very well. She likes him, they often talk together. He helped when she moved to new house. Brought his grandchildren to help, too. No problem. He's to retire soon."

"How about Nikhil Das? How do George and Nicky get along? Was there a problem between them?" I asked, just on the off chance. Feng stiffened, then shrugged. He wasn't telling. Of course I didn't press, just thanked him and left.

▲

MARCH IN SOUTHERN ONTARIO cannot make up its mind whether to stay winter or start being spring. On any given day it can be either. Or both. Today it was being end-of-winter-almost-spring. Of course this was a snare and an illusion; winter would return and the scenario would be played over again and again, each time a little closer to the real thing.

For now the sky was an innocent steel blue and there was more than a hint of sun's warmth in the air. Snow was gone from the lawns and sidewalks, leaving only the occasional blackened heap where the snowploughs had pushed it out of the way, uncovering mounds of dog turds and litter accumulated over the past four months. In sheltered nooks of the

Towers' grounds early shoots of brave crocus and iris peeked out at an unfriendly world. Driven by lengthening daylight, silhouettes of the trees had lost some of that sharp starkness of winter and were looking unmistakably fuzzy. Among the branches a blue jay, lively and splendid in its plumage, went on about its business.

A streetsweeper with a bunch of daffodils on the dashboard drove past cleaning out the gutters. The driver returned my wave. I stood out on the sidewalk in front of DP Towers, taking deep breaths, and watched his rear lights disappear up the street.

The media circus which attends every murder had gotten bored and moved on. For that moment the street was quiet, empty of traffic. Spring was in the air.

Walking around the perimeter of the Towers' property wasn't easy. In fact it was impossible. Past the front fence and the intrusive signboard with its pretentious announcements was a tall hoarding with Post No Bills in large stencilled letters. Scofflaws had covered it with posters, mostly concerned with selling something. This wall, dedicated to freedom of speech and profit, led me around the corner and down a short, narrow dead-end laneway. Closing off the bottom of the lane was a solid double gate locked with a padlock with a two-by-four board nailed across it for good measure. Private, No Admittance said a sign on the gate; another ordered hard hats to be worn. Clearly behind it was a construction site.

Promising myself to take a look at the site sometime from above — perhaps from one of the sixteenth floor apartments — I made for the employee parking lot and got the Escort on the road. In a few minutes I was heading south on Dufferin and back to Yorkdale Shopping Centre, from which there was no escaping in this part of the city.

Inside I let the warm, bright bustle enfold me. I walked slowly through the sparse early-afternoon crowds from one end of the giant indoor complex to the other. It's anchored by three major department stores, with names redolent of Canadian old money: Eaton's, Simpsons, and the Hudson's Bay Company. At The Bay I spotted Joyce Dossler with her son Norman, presumably doing some late March-break shopping. Young Dossler looked right past me while she smiled politely. They weren't interested in my company and vice versa.

After a stroll around The Bay I idled my way to a beer and sandwich.

I can't say that I was thinking about the Gurton case. I cannot say that I was thinking about much of anything. Yet it must have been percolating at some subliminal level because when I saw Rebecca Gurton coming out of one of the myriad chain clothing stores I was on to her like a flash.

"Well, hello there! Mrs. Rebecca Gurton, isn't it? I'm Helen Keremos. Remember me?" I knew damn well who it was and I would have bet she remembered me. Out of the goodness of my heart I wanted to give her a minute to collect herself. It can be disconcerting to be accosted in the middle of an impersonal place like a shopping mall. In the midst of the crowd the expectation is anonymity. I needn't have bothered.

"Yes, of course. Hello Helen."

Rebecca Gurton was a changed woman from the one I had first met just two nights ago. She was anything but mousy in the over-bright lights of Yorkdale, makeup, power dress, and all. It was a remarkably quick recovery from her husband's death.

"I am afraid I cannot stop to chat, I have an appointment. Perhaps some other time."

She smiled coolly, dismissively, and walked on by, leaving me standing there with my mouth open.

This was a bit much. Twice in one day I had been made to feel stupid! First Malory and now this bitch, Rebecca Gurton. I watched her disappear into the crowd and proceeded to follow. It wasn't hard. She cooperated, striding on, without looking to left or right, confident and purposeful. Shadowing is a snap in an uncrowded shopping mall designed to stream people into a few predetermined paths. Only the department stores have more than one entrance, for the most part what goes in must come out the same way. Rebecca Gurton didn't go into any of the stores. At least she wasn't lying about having an appointment. Without breaking step she walked into Joe Bird's bar and up to a table at which sat Mr. James Glendenning of Diamond Development Corporation.

Like a little gentleman he stood up, they shook hands and he helped her off with her coat. They sat down. Reflected through two sets of display windows, I watched them order from the menu, talking. I couldn't hear what was said but the picture was not one of perfect amity. Glendenning didn't look happy.

There was no point in spying on them any further. Anyway, they could see me if they took the trouble to look.

Walking away I thought I spotted a couple of plainclothes cops loitering with intent. One of them, presumably Glendenning's shadow, was in line for a frozen yogurt treat at the Diana Sweets' window. The other examined the window display at the Toys & Tots store opposite. He must have been following Rebecca Gurton right along with me! We made quite a tag team. Malory wasn't missing a trick. I wondered what he would make of this cozy tête-à-tête.

Back at the Towers I made straight for Clare Harwood's

office. I was determined; no more brush-off, I was in no mood to stand for it. I barged through the door without knocking. As soon as she saw me, Clare flew from her desk, pulled me into the room and closed the door, as if afraid I might escape.

"Oh, Helen, I'm so glad you're here at last! I've been looking all over for you. Where have you been? Never mind. We must talk."

There are days like that.

▲

"I FOUND HIM, Dennis Gurton ... dead, I mean," Clare Harwood was saying, holding on to me, our arms around each other in a monster hug. "Oh, Helen, it was terrible, terrible. I've never seen a dead body before. He was on the floor, looking just ghastly, ghastly ... and the smell! You know, shit."

She shuddered, her fingers digging into my back, her face hidden in my chest.

"And this was in the model suite, right? What made you go in there? Everyone thought you'd already left. Like George MacDonald," I said, trying to extricate myself gently.

There must have been a smidgen of skepticism in my voice, because she pulled away smartly, sat down, and buried her face in her hands.

"I told the police. A last-minute check, that's what it was. Before leaving. To make sure everything was —"

"Clare, you don't really expect Malory to buy that, do you? Late at night, just before you take off for a vacation with your kids you get the urge to check out a model suite which isn't going to be used before you get back anyway! And now you're going to tell me you moved the body into the empty apartment next door, right? And all by yourself, right? Spare me the histrionics."

"I don't care, I don't care! I knew the police wouldn't believe me, I didn't tell them about finding the body or any of that. But I thought you would, you must help me, Helen!"

"I didn't say I wouldn't help you, just that I don't think you're telling me the whole truth. I assume you went to that suite to meet Gurton. Well, what for? And you found him there dead. Why on earth did you move the body? And who else was there?"

Even as I formulated my questions I knew she wasn't about to give up her improbable story. Like a politician, Clare Harwood had learned the knack of ignoring inconvenient questions and sticking to her own agenda.

"I didn't want him found there, that's all. Model suite as the scene of a murder would be bad, very bad. So for business reasons I had to move the body. You wouldn't understand, you don't have to make your living being nice to people, making them feel good so you can sell them. Well, I do. It's my career, I have two children to support. I have to think of these things."

Cute how she managed to turn the subject around and away from the point at issue. I gave up.

"Okay. Just tell me your story. What you found in that apartment, how you managed to move the body, how much of all this you told the cops. And what you want me to do about it now."

It was her play, I didn't even remind her about the phone episode of the night before.

"He was right by the door, on the bedroom floor. Looking very dead. There was nobody else there. I looked. Nobody in the corridor, either. So ... so I got the cleaner's trolley from the service closet, and moved him, Dennis ... the body over to Apartment 1605. I had all my keys with me, you see. It seemed like a good idea. At the time."

She stopped, perhaps considering what she'd just said and whether it was going over.

"You picked up the body and put it on the trolley and then, still all alone, trundled it out of 1606 and down the hall to 1605, where you took it off the trolley and laid it out on the floor. I see. It must have been quite a strain. Nerve-wracking. And then what?"

Clare shrugged off my tone and stuck to her story.

"I put back the trolley, went back to 1606, and tidied up."

"What did you do about the smell?"

I didn't know whether to be amused or insulted by the number of unbelievable things I was expected to accept.

"Oh, the smell! Yes, we ... I ... had to get rid of it, so I struck a lot of matches and lit candles. That takes away the smell, you know. And the bed was disarranged, so I straightened that. I know I shouldn't have done that, clean up I mean. There might have been clues to the murderer. But I did it and now I cannot tell the police. They would never believe that I didn't kill him. And I didn't!"

Clare lifted her head. Her face seemed to confirm what she was saying. For sure some of it was true.

"No, they certainly wouldn't believe you if you told them this story. And I wouldn't blame them. But what makes you think they believe you now? All that phooey about happening to go up to the sixteenth floor to 'check' the model suite. Malory is sure you went up there to meet someone. Probably Gurton."

"I never saw him alive that night. And it doesn't matter what the police think as long as they cannot connect me to the murder. Isn't that so?"

She wasn't sure. In fact she was quite right. An unlikely but simple story which denies any involvement with the crime is hard to break. It's much easier to pry apart an "I was there and did all these things, *but* I am innocent." I could just hear Malory or, when it came to that, a Crown, asking Clare for exact details of her solo transportation of Gurton's body. Where did the matches and candles come from, what happened to the stubs? Not even a clever and experienced prevaricator like Clare Harwood would be able to keep her story from falling apart.

"Do you think I killed him? Don't you believe me?" She insisted on my commitment. I gave it some thought.

"No and no. I don't think you killed Gurton but I don't believe you, either. You were not alone, I'll bet on that. If you really disposed of Gurton's body as you say, someone helped you. You went up there to meet someone. Perhaps it was Gurton, perhaps not. Anyway, tell me more. What happened after you cleared up the stench in 1606? Where did you go?"

"Down to the second floor, like George says. It was bad luck he was in that elevator and remembered. It was a risk I had to take, going on the elevator. Using the fire stairs would have seemed very strange if I was seen by security. Being seen on an elevator would have been more normal, so less memorable all round. You see, by then everyone thought I was long gone.

I couldn't just walk out. So I had to hide overnight and sneak out in the morning."

Clare stopped and looked at me, as if trying to gauge my reaction to what she was about to say. Then she spoke quickly:

"Nicky was gone and you weren't moved in yet, so I spent the night in his apartment. And in the morning I went down to the garage and hid in the back of a car I knew would be driven out early. We drove to Yorkdale. Once the car was parked I got out and got a cab home, picked up my kids and my sister. Then we drove to the cottage, as planned."

"Without the car owner knowing you were there? Whose car was it?" I asked, amazed. This woman was quite something. I didn't know how much of this was true, if any, but regardless, Clare had some nerve. Even to be telling me this Hans Christian Andersen.

"Nobody knew, nobody saw me, nobody was with me the whole time. And I'm not saying another word. That's what happened. Period."

"I've heard more likely stories. But I'll give you this: it would be hard to disprove. So you may as well stick to it."

I was capitulating and not regretting it. Clare Harwood was shielding someone. Who was I, who had lied to the police on many occasions for just this reason, to tell her she couldn't? Much less that she shouldn't. Let's see her get away with it.

▲

IT WAS A PLAIN WHITE CARD, embossed with a coat of arms. On it, in black print, was an invitation to dinner with Eleena DeMoulard and Melhior Romulu at their suite number one thousand, six hundred and nine at twenty hundred hours that very day — all spelled out like that. Nothing so crude as a numeral. I accepted via the phone; there wasn't time to engrave it.

After my conversation with Clare I had a short, sharp parley with Malory, who wanted to know what she'd told me. I said "ask her" which didn't please him. In return he informed me that Das was still missing, that Tillion had an alibi of sorts, and that he, Malory, didn't need me to tell him about Clare because they, the police, had concluded that the murder had been committed in the number 1606 apartment, not 1605. Accordingly, Clare Harwood, who admitted being there, and Nicky Das, who was nowhere to be found, remained prime suspects, and what did I think of that? I said it was funny how his boys had missed spotting the model suite as the scene of the crime the first time they checked it, and wasn't it D'Arcy who'd been in charge of searching it? Malory tried not to grin. I followed up with how lucky that the police believed Clare's story or they would never have discovered where the crime had been committed. Malory found this less amusing. We parted friends, sort of.

Right then my main concern wasn't the murder. It was what to wear to the dinner at 1609. Not that I had much choice. My duffle didn't hold much; I'd been wearing my best threads for the past two days and my best weren't anything to brag about in any case. I wished I'd listened to Alice. She never tires of telling me to "get some decent clothes," by which she means trendy black Queen Street West stuff. I like it well enough and even own one or two pieces which are okay by her standards. But it all has to come together, and for me it never does.

Finally I settled for a fresh shirt with some silver jewellery borrowed from Das. I felt dressed up and that's what counts.

At 8:05 I was at the door of 1609. Too early of course, it's very middle class to be on time. Bourgeois. I couldn't help it, I was hungry. Eight o'clock is past my usual dinnertime.

The door opened. Not the door with 1609 on it but the numberless one next to it. I should have known evening meals would be served in the other suite, in the proper main dining room and not the morning room. When you live in a two-room apartment, it's hard to remember things like that.

The room I was led into by Mel Romulu was different. It wasn't colour coordinated like the place where I'd breakfasted the day before. It was a banal period piece instead. Oak and leather, green plush, and little brass studs on the chairs. Floor to ceiling morocco-bound books in dark oak bookcases, natch. Desk, a library table with *Architectural Digest, Country Living, The New Yorker* and what looked like old copies of *Punch*, at least half a dozen of the aforementioned straight-backed chairs, nicely worn oriental carpet of no particular distinction and a long buffet — oak — along one wall. A functioning fireplace with winged armchairs on either side, plus two slightly smaller club chairs, with attendant little side tables along the opposite wall. Unobtrusive brass lamps, indecipherable prints and maps on the walls, fresh flowers of large, bushy varieties in vases the size of laundry tubs. And over it all a chandelier, which I couldn't describe for any money, casting a pale, old-fashioned light.

"A drink?" Mel turned to me, raising his own glass with amber liquid in it. "I'm having rye and ginger."

Rye and ginger! There are certain things which speak of

traditional Canadian values and rye whisky with ginger ale is high on the list. It is so pre-boomer it could as well be mead. No middle-class urban Canadian under forty-five had even heard of such a drink, much less let it cross his lips.

"Sure," I said. "Why not rye and ginger."

"Good. It's the first drink I ever had in Canada. I started out in Hamilton in the fifties, when we still had a railroad industry, working at National Steel Car, making rolling stock. That's where I got a taste for rye and ginger. Until I entered dental school I thought that was the only thing Canadians drank, other than beer."

He handed me a glass. I brought it to my lips and took a fair swallow. Nostalgically pungent, sweet flavour flooded my taste buds. It suddenly occurred to me that Nick Das would not approve. Romulu indicated one of the armchairs at the fireplace. I sat down while he stood in front of me with one elbow on the mantelpiece. He would have been the picture of a perfect English squire at his hearth except for his clothes: a pyjamas-style suit in bright red satin and black cloth Chinese slippers. His jigsaw puzzle of a face looked white and drawn.

"Eleena will join us later," Romulu was saying. "Meanwhile we can graze. I hope you don't object to an informal self-serve supper like this."

He indicated the buffet laden with salads, cold cuts, breads, and relishes. Soggy potato salad, vinegary slaw, thinly sliced beef, chunks of canned ham, pieces of pale roast chicken, and a cruet stand with hot English mustard and three different types of relish. Bread and butter, salt and pepper. There were cups, sugar and milk, and a large silver teapot on the side. It perfectly matched the phony-Brit décor.

"What, no Marmite?" I said.

I got up and helped myself. Cutting up and eating food

from my lap is a skill I haven't bothered to acquire, so I pulled up a chair to the library table and fell to. Romulu nodded approvingly, filled his plate and joined me.

"Any progress with the murder?" he asked between bites.

I was to sing for my supper, as I had known all along. What other reason would Romulu have for my company?

"Couldn't say. You'll have to ask the police."

Romulu wiped his mouth with a napkin, sat back in his chair, picked up the glass of rye and ginger, turned, and aimed his out-sized eyebrows at me.

"Why so adversarial? Why not tell me what you know? And you do know quite a bit, I'll wager. I promise to reciprocate. We aren't on opposite sides."

"I don't know what side you're on. You tell me."

I kept on eating, ignoring the "said-the-spider-to-the-fly" atmosphere and the murder-game design of the room. I wondered whether Mel and Eleena kept a warehouse full of multifarious furniture somewhere from which to create backgrounds catering to their every whim. If so it seemed sad that they had nothing better to do with their money and time. Then I reminded myself not to be judgmental; who's to say what's a waste of life?

"You're a hard woman, Helen Keremos. That's good. We need someone like you who can minimize the damage the offical investigation will cause. No, don't interrupt. Since you won't talk to me, let me talk to you, for what it's worth. No strings."

"Talk away," I said.

"What we have here is a weak man with principles, a dangerous combination. This man wants to save the world, but over time he also begins to resent his wife's greater professional and especially financial success. We have a corporation whose well-being this weak, greedy man could affect. What would happen in such a case?" He paused, but it was a hypothetical question. "My take on Dennis Gurton is that he would be tempted. Now, you must realize that what he had for sale was no big deal in itself and very, very time limited. The strength of his position lay not in what he had as such but in the vulnerability of the corporation in question." Mel Romulu spoke with measured pomposity.

In spite of myself I was becoming interested.

"Oh?" I asked.

"Diamond Development Corporation is in financial trouble. Bad. This is no Cadillac Fairview or Olympia & York, you know, it's just one of dozens of little development companies which go belly-up every day. They've put everything into this development, Diamond Plaza Towers Phase I, and they absolutely need Phase II. Now Glendenning probably told you that a delay would cut into profits or something like that. But in fact a delay would kill Diamond Development Corporation."

"So what you're saying is that Gurton could've destroyed the corporation. How?"

"That's the kicker. He wouldn't have to do very much. Gurton's job for LWO was to research the utilization history of the site. These old airport lands had been in federal control for years; who knows what's been going on there since World War II? He was to find out what industry had used the location for what purpose in the past fifty years, at least. If he as much as found a smell of any industrial use which is connected with hazardous waste, like metal fabrication or an oil and coal plant, storage of old transformers, scrap metal yard, a tannery, or a thousand possibilities, it's game over for Diamond Development Corporation. It would mean serious environmental assessment and that can take years. Environmental testing alone of the soil for PCB's, mercury, lead, cadmium, and whatever, even if it ultimately gave the site a clean bill, would take too long. Too long for Glendenning and his partners to hold on and survive. They would lose DP Towers, their main asset."

"Just a minute. What you're saying is that Dennis Gurton didn't really need to know or have any evidence that the soil was contaminated. If he was able to even raise the possibility ... that would do it."

"Exactly."

"So he blackmailed Glendenning."

"Blackmailed! Of course not! Helen, you disappoint me. Blackmail doesn't enter into it. As soon as he started sniffing around he was given to understand that the corporation placed a high value on his cooperation."

"Oh, I like that! 'High value.' You're right, of course. It's not blackmail, it's bribery. Just one of the costs of doing business. Don't keep me in suspense. Did he bite?"

"At the time of his death it was still up in the air, as far as I know. Now that Gurton is dead, corporation management must try to do an end run around the whole matter, get the financing, pick up their option on the site, and get the building underway, before anyone else takes an interest and blows the whistle."

"Who actually owns the site as of this moment? Who had the smarts or luck to buy from the Feds one of the very few pieces of undeveloped land left in Metro Toronto? Present owners also have motive. So who are they?"

"A numbered Ontario company."

"And who owns the numbered company. Do you?"

I thought I had him, but he shook his head.

"No, I don't own it. It's part of the estate of the late Richard Dossler. My understanding is that it's the only substantial asset. And it's indeed substantial. Worth about twelve million dollars — conservatively."

"Well, well. So Joyce Dossler has a big fat motive."

"On the face of it yes, but not really."

"Why not? Think she's incapable of murder?"

"Nobody is incapable of murder. I think she was incapable of grasping the ramifications. On top of that she's got her hands full with that teenager of hers. Norman has taken his father's death very hard and takes it out on her. Joyce wouldn't be up to coping with an adolescent male even at the best of times. She considers the site already sold to Glendenning and is just waiting for probate to go through. According to her, it's all up to Glendenning and the Dossler lawyer."

Romulu rose, walked to the buffet, and replenished his glass. Walking back he gave me an encouraging smile.

"And her lawyer is Rebecca Gurton," I leapt in. This time I was on the button. "Which probably explains Glendenning and Gurton being chummy at Joe Bird's in Yorkdale this afternoon."

"Probably," Romulu said calmly, and sipped his drink, his mighty eyebrows raised as if in a question. "It strikes me as quite feasible that Rebecca as the grieving widow could manage to take-over Dennis' project and bury it. LWO is a largely volunteer organization, with a lot on its plate. It's likely no one would even notice."

For a moment we fell silent considering the possibilities and weighing the probabilities. I couldn't avoid feeling that Romulu knew too much about the game for a bystander. More like a player. Eventually I broke the silence.

"Fascinating, Mel. But where does all this get us? Assuming your information is correct, Joyce Dossler is out of it and Glendenning and his pals would have had a pretty good motive for doing away with Gurton *only* if he'd refused their kind offer, whatever it was. And you believe that he had succumbed to temptation, but you don't know for sure that that was the case. Right?"

"Right. Based on my analysis of his character, I say he persuaded himself that he wasn't betraying his principles by letting the transaction proceed, since there was no hard evidence of contamination on that property. He would rationalize that it wouldn't be fair to beggar DP Towers on the strength of an unsupported suspicion. A long shot for which they wouldn't be responsible in any case. And if DP Towers' managment, out of the goodness of their hearts, were to pay off the mortgage on his suite, well, that would be a nice birthday gift. And who would know? Except Rebecca, of course."

"Yes, Rebecca. She stood to gain both ways. As his wife and as the lawyer in the transaction. Conflict of interest in spades," I said. Then, remembering what Rebecca Gurton had blurted out when I first saw her on the night of Dennis' murder, I continued, "If you are right, then Glendenning had no good motive for murder. On the contrary his hope would be that Dennis Gurton stayed hale and hearty at least until Phase II was well underway. Same goes for Rebecca Gurton. And Joyce Dossler. No motive we know of. So, back to square one. And that is why you expect me to turn out my pockets for you, right, Mel?"

"Yes. That would indeed be much appreciated." As Mel Romulu spoke, the door opened and in walked Eleena DeMoulard. Giving me a smile, she walked up to Romulu and kissed him, stroking his forehead with one hand. He took the other in both of his and kissed her open palm. It was a totally spontaneous action, touching in its simplicity.

▲

ELEENA'S ARRIVAL DISRUPTED the dynamics between Mel and I somewhat more than usual when a third party joins an already functioning twosome. There was a shifting of seats in which I migrated back to the fireplace as Mel left the table to fuss over her. She didn't want any food, just a drink. A small glass of Amaretto in hand, she joined me in the other armchair while Mel took a stool by her side. All by itself this readjustment would have changed things, but somehow I did not feel that totally accounted for it. I'm not unduly sensitive to social dynamics but the difference in atmosphere was palpable.

Part of the reason was me. The brief hiatus gave me an opportunity to think about the conversation with Mel. About the implication of what he'd told me, about why I had been invited, and what his role was in all of this. He was curious about what I knew about the murder, fair enough. Fair enough also that he was interested in his neighbours and in the well-being of a company which managed the building in which he lived. But I couldn't help thinking that neither he nor Eleena were just neighbours with normal human curiosity. Instead of pumping me, as would have been most natural under the circumstances, so far he'd fed me information, the gist of which was that matters relating to DP Towers Phase II were not a motive for Gurton's murder. He'd done it all rather well, letting me come to this conclusion without having it spelled out and not pressing the point. Were I the suspicious sort, I would assume that he had an interest in protecting the corporation which owned DP Towers. Since *I am* the suspicious sort, that's exactly what I assumed.

That is not to say that I disbelieved him. Mel Romulu struck me as too intelligent a guy to tell lies. Partly because I flattered myself that he also didn't take me for a fool, partly because they weren't necessary. I believed that DP Towers was in financial trouble, I believed the Dossler estate owned the Phase II property, I believed that Dennis Gurton had the power to hurt the owners of DP Towers, I believed an attempt had been made to bribe him, I believed that Joyce Dossler wasn't directly involved. Even the business with Rebecca was all supposition but feasible ... so what was my problem with Mel's information?

All the above could be the truth, but it sure as hell wasn't the whole truth. There was something about the situation which escaped me so far, something which would change the picture substantially. Most probably this would be something which tied Mel and El directly into the murder. I could think of a number of possibilities which might more or less do this. The most obvious would be Mel's personal financial investment in DP Towers. Supposing he was one of its owners or at the very least a financial backer, mortgagee? He would stand to lose or gain right along with Glendenning and that gave him the same motive. Supposing Mel's reading of Gurton's character for my benefit was so much bullshit and Gurton had refused their bribe? Trouble was, even if that were true, I couldn't see Mel turning to murder. Not that he would have any scruples. But he was too smart to take the incalculable risk of taking Gurton out of the picture via murder. Murder tends to have uncontrollable consequences and murder focuses attention on the victim. And these are not outcomes that anyone with an interest in DP Towers would have wanted. QED — that line of reasoning also took Mel off the hook. Unless his motive was personal and had nothing to do with DP Towers, which brought my attention back to Eleena DeMoulard.

I looked at her as she sat deep in the chair with her hand in Mel's, sipping her drink and gazing into the fire. Tonight she wasn't dressed for any part, unlike Mel. She wore blue jeans with a simple sportshirt and running shoes. It did nothing to detract from her beauty. Sprawled in the chair with natural grace, fire reflecting on her bronze skin, she was a woman people would kill for. Her face and body glowed with the well-being which comes to those who love and are loved. That she was the object of Mel's love there could be no doubt. But was he the object of hers? Supposing ...

"What were you two talking about before I arrived? Something about this awful murder, of course I know that. But what? Helen, anything new?" Eleena brought the conversation back to the topic which was on all our minds. Mel immediately answered for me.

"Helen was just about to tell all, weren't you, Helen? I'd already filled her ear with everything we know about Dennis and the Phase II situation. So it's her turn."

Both of them turned to me inquiringly. I plunged in.

"Here is a piece of news for you. It's about Clare Harwood. Apparently she was around until quite late on the night of the murder. George MacDonald saw her take the elevator down from this floor at close to eleven o'clock. She told the police she'd been up checking the model suite. Of course, they don't believe her. What is more, Malory has now established to his satisfaction that Gurton wasn't killed where his body was found, in Apartment 1605. Now he's sure it was really 1606, where Clare has admitted being near the time of the murder. Malory is only looking for a motive and possibly for an accomplice. Nicky Das makes the perfect candidate for that since he is still missing and cannot account for himself. What d'you think of that for a story-and-a-half?"

"Oh, poor Clare, how awful for her! Why would she want to kill Dennis? It doesn't make sense. Do you think they'll arrest her?" Eleena's reaction seemed a little forced.

"I agree, it doesn't make sense. What d'you think Helen, can they prove that Dennis died in 1606? Are they claiming Clare moved his body? With Nick Das? It's absurd!" Mel's reaction was no less strong. My news about Clare Harwood appeared to have shocked them both. The murder of Dennis Gurton had been transformed from a topic of keen but academic interest into a matter of considerable concern.

"I don't know what they can prove. It wouldn't be easy to prove where the murder actually took place unless they found a lot of physical evidence. Which is doubtful. As for Clare moving the body, again my guess is it would be hard to prove unless there is a witness. Let's say the accomplice turns Crown witness — assuming there is an accomplice and assuming Clare is really involved. She hasn't admitted any of this to the police."

I spelled it all out carefully and waited. Eleena took the bait.

"Do you think that whoever moved the body was also the murderer? You said the police suspected Nick Das. Do they think that he murdered Dennis in 1606 and then got Clare to help him move the body to the other suite?"

"I think that right now that is their favourite hypothesis. Which they will pursue unless and until something happens to discredit it. I don't think they have enough on Clare to arrest her, but any way you cut it she is in for a very unpleasant time. And Nick Das as well, once they catch up with him. Any idea where Das might have disappeared to? Any guesses?"

Unintentionally I addressed my question to Romulu.

"I've been thinking about that and I must say Nick's disappearance seems quite inexplicable. I know he was anxious to get to India, both worried and excited about it. Hmm, it's a puzzlement."

Mel Romulu moved away from Eleena and took up his stand at the mantelpiece again, looking down on the two of us.

"How well did you get to know him?" I asked, remembering Nick's rather lofty reaction to Romulu and DeMoulard's vanity plates. "How did you get along?"

"You know, it's just occurred to me, but he and I had quite a complex relationship. Das always struck me as a very fine, very worthwhile, and very unhappy man. I think he couldn't come to terms with his background, he wasn't sure who he was, somehow. He has this passion for all things British, yet he hates India's colonial past. About independent India he's always seemed to me to be like a disappointed lover: bitter that the promise of independence hasn't been fulfilled. He deeply despises Indian politicians and the new middle class. A bit of an elitist is Nick. You know, he was born on the very day India became independent and it seems to have affected his whole life. Or perhaps all Indians of his class and generation have this ambivalence about their country and the old Raj, I really don't know." Mel paused and then continued with a reminiscent smile, "He and I had a lot in common, both being immigrants to Canada. I would tease him about how easy it must have been for him, an adult, well educated and native English speaking. Compared with the likes of me, arriving in 1956 with no money, no English and no education of the sort which counts over here. He would get quite irate and tell me that I couldn't imagine how colour conscious white Canadians were because it was outside my experience. I remember once he accused me of being colour-blind! Of only seeing bigotry and discrimination on the basis of religion or language or ethnic origin. The way it is in Central Europe where historically neighbours fight neighbours, and imperial masters colonize their next-door cousins. He used to say that I didn't understand how the British treated their colonies. We had many arguments about that. He said once, 'You think of me as you would of an English gentleman, but no English gentleman would ever make that mistake.' He was right, of course."

"You don't know any English gentlemen, Mel, so how can you tell! This is all so past tense, I cannot believe it. Who cares about the British Raj or imperialism or all that stuff. It's history. I think Nicky is a sweet man but totally out of it. Victorian, really. He doesn't belong to the here and now and I don't think he belongs anywhere in this world," Eleena interpolated vehemently.

"Eleena *is* right. The most crucial thing about Nicky is certainly not his race but his old-school values. He's attached to things that were considered unfashionable by the time he was born. Like classical education. For instance, he believes in loyalty, formal manners, and chivalry towards women. Didn't you notice, Helen?" Mel asked.

"I only met him once and that only briefly. He struck me as an old-style professional, hard working, organized, and knowledgeable about his job. As it happens these are qualities

I admire. On the downside, I would put him down as a bit compulsive, a perfectionist, a workaholic probably."

"Own up, Mel. You often complained what a stuffy bore Nick Das could be. And you were insufferable around him. You gave the poor guy a hard time at every opportunity. You cannot deny it!"

Eleena spoke to Mel without looking up from the fire. She seemed to be using our discussion of Nick Das to attack Mel. It was a dynamic between them to which I wasn't privy. Mel took it calmly.

"I don't deny it. In many ways he is a stuffy bore and highly deserved having the piss taken out of him. Nevertheless I like him. He took my teasing in good part. It did him good. Many people were uncomfortable around him, he didn't seem to have any close friends. He and I played chess and talked as equals. I miss him. And I don't believe for a minute that he murdered Dennis Gurton. And supposing he had. If Clare was his accomplice, then he would never have left her to face the police alone. That's not the Nick Das I know."

"That sort of leaves you two, you know that? You've just about eliminated everyone else!" I said.

"Now, now, Helen! This isn't a locked-room mystery. No such thing! Surely it could be anybody in the building, and in fact it could be anybody, period. You aren't going to claim that our security can keep out anyone who really wants to get in, are you?" Mel sounded interested.

"It's not what I claim, it's what the cops think that matters. And they are seriously concentrating only on people on this floor plus the staff. No one else in the whole complex appears to have had any connection with Dennis Gurton or even knew him to speak to. As for outsiders, well, that's what Glendenning would like it to be, not surprisingly. He would prefer that Gurton was killed by the proverbial prowler, even thought it would reflect badly on building security. But you cannot expect anyone else to take that as a serious probability. As I said, once everyone else is out of it, it leaves you two."

We batted this idea around for a while but neither Eleena nor Melhior took it sufficiently seriously to get defensive and spill anything they might have to spill.

At eleven I made a move to leave. I said goodbye to Mel, still standing and on his fourth rye and ginger, moodily looking into the fire.

Eleena took me to the door and followed me out into the hall. Impulsively she kissed me on the cheek, pressed my shoulder, and said, "I'm so glad you're here. Clare has such faith in you, I know you won't let her down. Good night."

Interesting, eh? I asked myself on my way down to Das' apartment. With too much to think about I fell asleep instantly, without even calling Alice.

▲

"HALLO, SWEETIE!"

Alice's voice came across the line clear and strong. It was late morning and I hadn't expected to find her at home.

"Well, this is a shock. I wanted to speak to a machine and instead I get a real human being. I think I'll hang up and try again," I said. Alice laughed.

"Disappointed, eh. Sorry about that. Anything new?"

She meant about the murder, of course. I didn't feel like talking about it right then.

"I'll tell you when I see you."

" Yeah? And when will that be? Can you stay over tonight?"

" If you ask me nicely. Anything new your end? Have you been discovered yet?"

"Consider yourself asked. Nothing new ... Oh, yes ... you got a call from Nate. He left a number. That would be Nate Ottoline, your old buddy, I expect. I'd love to meet him."

"That's great, good old Nate! I'd been trying to find him since I got here. He'd moved and gotten an unlisted number. I left messages for him all over the place. I guess one of them reached him. Yes, of course, let's all get together. Gimme that number, I'll call him right away."

"Okay but be sure and call me right back."

"Done."

I called the number Alice had given me. A sleepy voice answered. Unmistakeably Nate Ottoline! "Well, Helen, at last! It's been years, you know that? What are you doing in town? Still detecting?"

"You could say that. Never mind, tell you all about it when I see you. How's by you?"

"Oh, not too badly, everything considered."

"Good. Let's get together soon. Sooner. Soonest. When?"

" Hey, it's been years since anybody's been that excited to meet with me! Does this old heart good. I'm free tonight, how about it? Do I get to meet your girlfriend? Alice, is it?"

"You're free tonight, at a moment's notice? Things have changed. But that's great, and yes, I'll bring Alice. Where and when? Where do you hang out these days?"

"Let's meet at the Bamboo on Queen Street. About 8 p.m. if that suits you."

"Fine, see you there."

"Good. Till then, then. Bye."

I put down the receiver slowly, still hearing Nate's familiar voice, and thought about how much older we were now, both of us, and how changed from when we first met.

That was during the Martin Millwell case, when we started out as adversaries and ended up allies. Our frienship grew after that in spite of our differences and Nate helped me out again over Sonia Deerfield's problems.

Our friendship was an unlikely one. In those days Nate Ottoline was a rather sleazy operator in the pre-AIDS gay community in Toronto. At one time or another he owned after-hours drinking clubs, produced porno movies, promoted young male studs, laundered drug money, and probably did other things I am pleased not to know about.

Nate and Ronnie, his houseman and sometime lover, lived very well on the considerable cash flow from all these questionable enterprises. They had an expensive apartment at the Colonnade on Bloor Street West, they wore expensive suits, smoked expensive cigars, and drank expensive booze. They snorted the best coke and fucked the most beautiful young men. Not exactly desirable citizens by most standards, not even by mine.

My life-style at that time could also be described as sleazy, but in another sense. I made my living hand-to-mouth as a freelance private investigator in Vancouver. It meant a lot of hanging around street corners, hotel lobbies, and race tracks, watching people who owed other people money or who might be talking to competitors or who were making out with other people's spouses. Big-time stuff, eh. The work wasn't very lucrative even when there was work. Too often it was a long time between pay cheques and I had to scramble to make rent on my third-floor walk-up over a Kwick Print store just a bottle throw from Hastings and Main. I drove a GMC van, wore jeans, and drank beer. When I got lucky I smoked a little weed and made love with women I'd picked up in bars. That was the seventies; an exciting time but not necessarily a stage in my life I would want to revisit.

By the time of my involvement with Sonia Deerfield, things had picked up a bit. I was getting a higher class of work, better paid and more regular. I could afford a fancy off-the-road 4x4 with all the glitzy extras. When over the course of the case it went *boom*, insurance replaced it. By the time Sonia and I hit West Coast La-La-land there was still seven thousand dollars in the bank.

When Sonia and I parted, I went back to Vancouver in time for Expo 86. My building got "redeveloped," but business did improve. I had a spacious basement, with private entrance near the fish plants on Powell. I drove a plush minivan, wore pants with pleats and oversize jackets with shoulder pads. I belonged to a food co-op, bought recycled toilet paper and bottled water, took vitamins. Smoking dope gave me headaches.

Some things hadn't changed, however. My preference still was for beer and bright, sexy women. I still thought that "going into" therapy was a boring way to spend discretionary income, if any.

Given all those changes I'd gone through, I wondered how Nate was faring in the nineties. I was soon to find out.

I called back Alice and we agreed I'd come to her apartment about 6 p.m., and we would make our meet with Nate together.

▲

FULL OF ANTICIPATION for my evening to come with Alice and Nate, I contemplated the long day before me. I would have been happy to forget the murder, DP Tower, and my job, and spend the rest of the day with my feet up reading a book, or doing something else constructive. But it was not to be. Malory was on the prowl. He cornered me in the office and proceeded to tell me his troubles.

Things were not going very well. Malory didn't say so in so many words but he and his minions hadn't gotten anywhere. The list of where they hadn't gotten was lengthy.

"Take your friend Clare Harwood, please! She's lying but she's good at it. D'Arcy and I have taken turns at her and we can't shake her. The super — remember Superintendent Sterling — well, he's moved on to greener pastures. The new super is a hard nut, won't let us arrest her unless we can make a case. He wants to have chapter and verse — you know — who, when, how, why. We can make guesses at some of it, the problem is we have half-a-dozen scenarios, each equally likely."

Malory shook his head in frustration, looking discouraged and worried. Some of it was likely real this time and some of it was grandstanding. Hard to tell the difference with a guy like Malory.

"Or equally unlikely. So what's your favourite right now? Clare Harwood and who else?" I asked.

"I don't have any favourites, but I'll give you D'Arcy's if you like. It's Clare Harwood and Nick Das having a hot and very hush-hush affair. We really pumped the staff downstairs and it appears that Clare used to go up to the model suite more often than seemed strictly necessary. Using it as a second office when she wanted to get away from the phone was how she explained it. Das' movements we cannot pin down so well. He doesn't keep office hours and no one keeps track of him. But it makes sense, that place is perfect for a quick fuck. The bed had been used, if you take my meaning and we found evidence of candles and some sweet beverage. So D'Arcy sees Das as murderer Number One and Harwood as a kind of Lady Macbeth or perhaps only a witness and accomplice, it doesn't matter which. As for motive, we don't need anything complex. Suppose Gurton caught them at it somehow, Das karate chopped him dead. D'Arcy's sure Das is trained in martial arts. We aren't saying it was premeditated, could be just an accident. For one reason or another they decided not to report Gurton's death — don't blame them really — packed the body over to the empty suite next door to throw us off the scent. Something like that is quite feasible. It bugs my ass that we cannot find this Das character. Once we get our hands on him we can arrest them both and break them apart, I know we can. D'Arcy has wasted hours, damn it, going through Das' things looking for a lead. Nothing."

"What about forensics?"

"Ah, forensics. Sometimes I think we were better off without all this science crap. We need to know how Gurton was killed, right? Well, these wise guys will not just say they don't know, they cover ass for pages and pages. 'Consistent with,' 'some evidence points to,' 'it is not unlikely that' — you know their shtick. All we know for sure is that his Adam's apple was crushed. Karate chop? Could be. A blow, or blows, from a rigid narrow object — like a steel bar or even the edge of a book? Could be. They won't exclude it. What does it get us? Zip." Malory sighed, "Helen, have you got any ideas?"

The question amounted to quite an admission for Malory to make. He needed help. He didn't like D'Arcy's scenario — hell, he didn't like D'Arcy — but he couldn't come up with anything better. Five days after the murder the pressure was on and they couldn't even find one of their chief suspects! No wonder Malory was sitting in my — Das' — office, squirming in his chair, asking me for ideas. I loved it.

"Tell me, what about other possibilities? Who had a real live motive to eliminate Dennis Gurton? How about the widow? Romulu and DeMoulard, any motive there? Dossler and Glendenning had motives, what did you do about that? This man Tillion has an alibi, does he?"

"I wish he didn't. But give me credit, eh. Rebecca Gurton is a prime suspect, spouses always are. She's in one of the possible scenarios D'Arcy and I have been trying on for size. It goes like this: Harwood and Gurton are lovers, his wife catches them, there is a struggle, he gets killed, the two women move the body to cover the whole affair. Stranger things have happened but I don't for a minute believe in this one. And don't think it hasn't occurred to me that it's the two women who were lovers. But it doesn't work. For one thing, Harwood used to go up there during office hours when neither of the Gurtons were around. Next, take the sex triangle out of it, and Rebecca Gurton may have a mint of financial reasons to get rid of her old man. But in that case, where do the model suite and Clare Harwood come in? And where is Das! Too damn many loose ends and no satisfactory answers to anything."

"All right. How about the other couple on that floor? What's their interest in the Gurtons, if any?"

"You mean the circus act of Romulu and DeMoulard? He's loaded. People's teeth are a gold mine. Some of those dentists make more money in a week than we see in a year. Then he was smart, invested well, real estate mostly, didn't fall for any boiler-room scams like so many do. He quit dentistry, lives on just a fraction of his income, invests, plays games, travels. Not a bad life. Never married. They've been together for about three years. Eleena DeMoulard, very continental. That's a laugh, she's from Shawinigan, Quebec. Father and mother both schoolteachers. She trained in a nursery, the greenhouse kind, not the kind with kids. Went to a community college, whatever they call them there, moved to Quebec City, worked in a flower shop. Must have met Romulu there. She's twenty-four. That's all we know about her, other than what you can see just by looking at them."

"So you cannot connect then to the Gurtons or DP Towers?"

"Oh, he has some interest in this development, mostly because he owns those two suites they live in. Naturally he wants the project to be well managed, properly registered, and so forth. But no major financial involvement that we can trace. It's always possible, of course. About the Gurtons and this LWO business, it's even harder to pin down. Both Romulu and

DeMoulard are environmental activists of a kind. You know, those people with no jobs to worry about and time on their hands. Romulu is on the LWO mailing list, we checked. Both of them were up in Temagami decorating trees or something, at one time. Apparently they left when some other demonstrators didn't take to them. Too weird even for eco-nuts, I guess."

"That's all you've got?"

"You kidding! I've got so much data, information, reports, and assorted stuff, a thousand trees must have died to supply the paper it's on. You want more bits and pieces? See what you make of this: Romulu and Das played chess together; Dennis Gurton had a bunch of porno magazines hidden in his office; we found a copy of the Ontario Spills Bill in Das' apartment — that's the law on hazardous waste in this jurisdiction; this building has the best security system available and the staff is considered first-rate; we got hold of a file which Wayne Tillion gave to Glendenning on what Gurton claimed to have found out about the Phase II property. You follow? Well, it talks about possible storage of PBB's — that's polybrominated bi-phenyls, don't feel bad, I didn't know, either — a fire retardant. Nothing specific, no sources, no evidence. Nobody can tell me what it means, if anything. Norman Dossler has a crush on Eleena D.; he insists that Melhior Romulu is a fag and Dennis Gurton was his lover. Now get this, George MacDonald claims that Nihil Das' father was a traitor in World War II. Says Das Senior was an officer in the Indian army who as a POW in Burma cooperated with the Japanese. Eleena is planning to open an interior decorating business; she designed their apartment, but Romulu shelled out for it ... That's just the tip of the iceberg. You want more, I'll give you more."

Malory looked triumphant as if he'd done something clever. Poor sod. I almost felt sorry for him.

"Some of these facts have nothing to do with the murder, but some of them might. You cannot tell the wheat from the chaff. No wonder. To find out which is which you need a hypothesis that works. And you don't got one," I responded with the obvious.

"Tell me something I don't know. Let's face it, I was hoping you would."

Malory made himself sound dejected. It was a con but so what.

"Spare me. Okay, let's start with the assumption that the murderer and the body mover were different people, possibly totally unconnected," I said, watching Malory watching me.

"So that's what Harwood told you! That she moved the body but didn't waste Gurton. Consider it assumed. What next?"

"Discount Nick Das as the murderer. In fact, think of him as out of it."

"That's difficult."

"Try."

"Right. We have a murderer, unknown except that it's not our best suspects, Harwood or Das! We have Harwood and a person unknown, except that it's not Das, moving the body from Suite 1605 to 1606. So I'm left with no suspects and no motive. Gimme a break! Where does that leave me?"

"Closer to the truth, that's all. That should be worth something."

Malory shrugged and pretended to be disappointed. In fact, he'd more or less found out what Clare had told me and generally gotten a fresh view of the case, which is what he'd come to me for in the first place. I didn't begrudge him any of it.

▲

BY 5 P.M. I WAS CHAMPING at the bit to be away from there, on the way downtown to Alice and Nate. I'd done my rounds, pretended to be busy with my security job. To give my mind something more interesting to chew on I went up to the sixteenth floor, and ignoring the yellow scene-of-the-crime tapes, busted into Suite 1606. Through the southeast window I didn't need to crane my neck very far to locate the fence and gate to the adjacent site which I took to be the Phase II property that all the fuss was about. On the site itself was a mess of semidemolished small, decrepit industrial buildings, prefabricated sheds and the like. A backhoe had wreaked havoc amongst them, churning up the paved roadway, piling up old lumber, sheets of roofing material, rusty cisterns, pipes, and other industrial scrap into untidy heaps. To date not much had been done to clear the site or prepare it for construction. I guessed that that would start once Diamond Development Corporation had title to the property, assuming they could get it.

This potential DP Towers Phase II site abutted on the landscaped grounds of Phase I, from which it was separated only by a three-foot high wrought-iron fence. The high hoarding with the gate, which I had examined the day before from the street, enclosed both properties together. No wonder Joyce Dossler was sure the sale was a fait accompli. Just looking down on the two properties together made it easy to take for granted. The visual message was all the stronger for being subliminal.

Deep in thought I made my way downstairs, ready to pick up my jacket in the office and be on my way out. The lobby was relatively busy with people coming home from work, or on their way to the squash courts. Sneaking out without encountering anyone wasn't going to be easy. And for once that day I was right. Just out of my office I virtually stumbled into Rebecca Gurton, accompanied by a middle-aged gentleman in a dark suit, and by Wayne Tillion. He gave me another of his patented dirty looks and tried to keep her moving past me. Remembering how she brushed me off at Yorkdale the other day got me mad enough to want to pay her back a little. Everyone gets childish like that on occasion. So I grabbed her arm, swung her around to face me, and demanded loudly:

"What about that automobile accident your late husband had just before he died? Sure that wasn't another attempt on his life? How about letting us in on that, Mrs. Gurton, eh?"

It just came out like that, with no premeditation on my part. I mean, I had no idea what I was going to say until it came out of my mouth. I love that old unconscious, it keeps on working no matter what. And I loved that the stunned Rebecca Gurton replied:

"What? What accident? Oh, that! That was nothing. Dennis scraped a fender, trying to avoid hitting a bike. That's all. Now leave me alone, you've got no business making allegations like that."

She flounced off towards the elevators, with everyone in the lobby looking after her. Grinning happily I made for the outside doors, exchanging nods and waves with my audience. There was Sam Feng, ramrod solid, an uncomprehending Joyce Dossler and her wide-eyed son, a worried Clare Harwood with Francis Malory looking daggers at me over her shoulder. What did I know about that accident that he didn't, and why didn't I tell him? is what he's thinking, I bet. Plus an assorted bunch of fascinated bystanders whom I don't know but who will know me after this.

The day was getting better and better. Alice was home and glad to see me. The moment I was in the door she was all attentive and affectionate. Fact is I couldn't remember the last time she'd been this way since I arrived in Toronto. Sex was one thing, but it was that everyday love and concern that had been missing. So we took a little time for some good old-fashioned smooching. Very nice. My moving out had done its magic.

We didn't talk much. I gave her the highlights of the doings at DP Towers, she filled me in a bit on her last few days in the esoteric world of theatre.

Mostly I watched her prepare for a night out on the Queen West strip. There is something about a beautiful woman in a bathtub which ... well, there is something about it.

She took her time washing, drying, and working on her hair. Wet, it tends to go into tight curls which in my náiveté I thought was trendy these days, but apparently they were the wrong sort of curls. How do people know what's trendy on any given day? Whenever I ask Alice about it she just smiles and tells me to look at people on the street. It has to be the right people on the right streets, mind you. So to begin with you have to know which people on which streets. How? And how do they know what's really, really trendsetting and what's merely fashionably commercial and already passé for folks who care about these things? I guess it's like perfect pitch. Either you have it or you don't.

Alice in her evening-out gear: black tights, short leather skirt which barely covers her kiester. Black, of course. A flowered top very showy and colourful. Lots of jewellery on ears, neck, fingers, all over. Black patent leather pumps. She threw on a cape; the evening was cool. She looked me over critically; my best peg-leg pants, white linen shirt, red embroidered vest. I would do. We were on our way to see ol' Nate.

▲

WE DECIDED TO WALK SOUTH to Queen. It was Friday night in late March, just getting dark. Me and Alice in our best, walking down Spadina, my favourite street in Toronto. Life should be like this all the time, except if it were, we wouldn't appreciate it. I was appreciating it. It was a change from the burbs and all those people worried about the price of condos.

We started on the east side of Spadina, past Chinese and Vietnamese restaurants wedged among a rash of cash-and-carry wholesalers of assorted junk. Sunglasses, costume jewellery and findings, plastic toys, digital watches at $2.99 ...

Gentrification is still minimal around there; the only veggie café for blocks and the one true antique store don't seem to be doing much business. Grossman's Tavern, looking unchanged since the sixties — was that possible ? — is still there, but in the next block a provincial liquor outlet decked out in fancy tiles sits where the scuzzy Paramount Tavern used to be.

Each side of Spadina is different. On this stretch the west side is busier, people pouring out of the side streets from busy Kensington Market and shopping at the houseware, yard-goods, and discount variety stores. All the Jewish restaurants and Hungarian butchers are long gone, replaced by their Asian equivalents. Farther south there are parts of blocks which seem solidly by and for Koreans or by and for Chinese or Vietnamese, but here there is still a mix of storekeepers catering to a mix of customers. There are faces of every shade, the street smells of Peking duck and the music in the air is reggae.

Dundas Street east of University Avenue used to be Toronto's only Chinatown. Now the corner of Spadina and Dundas is the centre of one of a number of Chinatowns in Toronto. Banks on all four corners advertise aggressively in four languages — none of them French. Fresh produce spills out onto the side-walks: baskets, boxes, bundles full of familiar and unfamiliar vegetables, fruit, and fish. Crowds, noise, garbage, but it is still Toronto. A Green Hornet walks calmly through the chaos, ticketing illegally parked vehicles blocking laneways, straddling sidewalks.

The character of the street starts to change after that with the "Fashion District," which is just an upscale term for the schmatta business, taking over from the jumble of Chinatown. Buildings grow taller with manufacturers and brand names up on the windows, six, seven stories above the jammed street.

There is a little store-front retail action in discount and high-fashion furs but it isn't nearly as lively as the area farther north which we had just passed through.

Then it was Queen Street, and Alice almost dragged me under a red streetcar to talk to a friend. Nobody I knew, but after just a few months in Toronto Alice knew more people here than lived in all of Vancouver. Or so it seemed to me. I was introduced, I was given the once over, I was a hit! I didn't know that older women were "in" but it was nice to hear.

East of Spadina, where Queen Street widens is still the heart of the strip. This used to be artists' country. They moved in, made it interesting, and raised property values. Now purists who despised the commercial exploitation and chain boutiques were moving west of Bathurst to escape high rents. Still, here was where cool, funky people came to see and be seen. Walking with Alice, I felt like that's us.

The entrance to the Bamboo is a narrow passage between two stores barred by a glass booth, like in a parking lot. Inside the booth was a large smiling man who wanted ten dollars from each of us. I almost had a bird. Alice told me to be cool. It wasn't a cover. We'd get it back if we didn't stay for the show which started at 10 p.m. The smiling dude said "have a nice dinner" as if he meant it — I kid you not — and we passed through the courtyard into a space like a bus barn converted into a "venue" — food, liquor, music, performance. It was large, noisy, dark, and full of people and smoke.

Alice entered into negotiations with a tiny, beautiful woman in a sari who controlled the dinner tables. I looked around. The bar was packed three deep, and it was only just 8 p.m. All the tables were full and there were people, mostly women, sitting on Salvation Army couches near the entrance, waiting. The cacophony was extraordinary considering that the stage was empty; all this noise was just people talking to each other. I hated to think of the decibels once the music started. Must be something about the accoustics in this place.

I grabbed a small table near the bar and ordered a beer while Alice continued to try for a table in the dining room. Insects, palms, and red light bulbs predominated in the bar décor. There can't be many drinking establishments with a cockroach the size of a Jeep in green and red primary colours on the wall. If there were, I'd been missing them.

It was a high energy place; I liked the buzz. But I knew I wouldn't be able to hack it for long. Unlike the younger generation around me, I still have unimpaired hearing and would prefer to keep it that way.

There was no sign of Nate but Alice returned triumphant, having managed to get her name on a waiting list for a table in the dining room. She promised me that it would be quieter there and that I'd like the food.

The Bamboo clientele was a mixed lot, nothing special. Mostly young of course but not obnoxiously so. The staff moved on the jump, fast and keen like they all had a feather or something up the ass. It could be just hormones and dedication.

To pass the time I asked Alice if she knew what Bamboo's hiring policy might be; she looked at me suspiciously but didn't get it. By me, the male servers were all large, wore Doc Marten boots and either ponytails or dreadlocks, while the female staff were all small, gorgeous, and done up to the nines. Could that be coincidence, I asked Alice again? This time she laughed. All was well.

Quarter of an hour went by. No Nate, no table for dinner. I went to get some nibbles at the take-out counter. And there was Nate plunking loonies into a Match-Mate video machine!

"Well, lordsy me! If it isn't the Great Ottoline! No wonder we couldn't find you. What are you doing hiding next to the popcorn?"

"Helen! Let's look at you. God, it's good to see you. My, my, we're looking spruce."

Hugs and kisses. We held each other at arm's length and checked. He was older but then who wasn't? Still a snappy dresser, no expense spared. I'm not sure what he saw looking at me, but it seemed to be all right.

"Where's Alice? Lead me to her. I want to meet 'the woman who.' "

"Little table near the bar. See if you can find her, guess who she is. I've got to get us some nosh before we expire from the hungers."

"You do that, while I finish with this bigoted hetero game. See, when you identify yourself as a male then all your mates are female. And vice versa, natch. So I've had to lie about my gender to get any answers I can live with. Height of discrimination! I should complain to the management."

Out of the corner of my eye I watched the woman behind the counter. She was young and not at all sure how to react to Nate. Is he serious or what? I bought some nachos and we walked away.

"How come you picked this place to meet and not some gay bar? Where Match-Mate games are for real," I asked, munching.

"Yeah. That's a good reason right there. Besides, I live around here now, on McCaul, it's home turf. All the best gay bars, at least those I like, are east of Yonge. Hey, I bet that's Alice!" And Nate made straight for Alice.

She took one look at this stranger advancing towards her, stood up, and opened her arms. It did my heart good to watch them hug.

I went to scrounge up another chair while Alice and Nate got acquainted. It took me a while what with one thing and another. By the time I got back they were deep in conversation; the topic was postmodernism. I don't know from modernism, never mind "post" so I could not contribute. I sat and admired the erudition around me. Seemed there was a new book on the politics of postmodernism which neither had read. That was a lot to have in common, right there.

Time passed, no table for dinner materialized ...

"Alice, how about checking our table reservation, eh? We've been waiting forty minutes. Enough already."

Alice nodded and took off. Nate and I watched her as she strode towards the little podium by the door from where dinner tables were dispensed to those judged worthy.

"Well?" I asked.

"Well, indeed. Far out, as we used to say. Congratulations, Helen, she's splendid."

"Yeah, I think so, too."

"But will this relationship keep you in town with her?"

"No," I had to admit.

"Hmm."

Alice was back. She picked up her cape and flung it on.

"Let's go. We missed our table, it seems. She says she called my name and we didn't answer. So we missed our turn. Let's get outta here."

"You're putting me on! She told you that she called your name, in this racket? Yeah, let's get our dough back and go somewhere else. That okay by you, Nate?"

The three of us made our way out the door while people pushed past us to get in, asking for tables.

Down the street we tried Le Select Bistro. No bus barn this. Uptown place freshly done up in dark wood, lots of glass and mirrors. We got a table in the back and large menus in French with English subtitles. Along came an attentive waiter and very soon a bottle of wine. Finally!

▲

"How come none of that lot cares whether there really is hazardous waste on the Dossler property? I would think someone would take the possibility seriously, don't you?"

We'd ordered and started on the wine and the bread which lived in little baskets suspended on pulleys above our heads. To make room for food on the bistro-size tables, I guessed. Anyway, it was cute.

Alice proceeded to tell Nate the story of my job at DP Towers and the murder. He'd read about it in the *Toronto Star* and listened to her very accurate account with interest.

Nate had lost some weight, so that his face now drooped a little, showing his age, which must be close to fifty. He still wore his hair short and his moustache drooped. I missed the cigar and the sharp look in his dark eyes which had been such integral parts of his personality. This was a softer, mellower Nate Ottoline. Perhaps also sadder, it occurred to me.

Now I had to concentrate on an answer to Alice's question. There was something in what she said but I felt like pontificating instead of thinking about it.

"These days it's either apathy or panic about anything to do with pollution. Unless you are going to live there, why should you care about the possibility of hazards on that property? And what would be the significance of caring as far as the murder is concerned? There is too much else unexplained about the situation at the Towers. Let me just tell you what else Malory told me today."

I went on to describe blow by blow my conversation with Malory and my subsequent byplay with Rebecca Gurton in the lobby. Alice and Nate listen avidly.

After I'd finished Nate said, "I bet you have a hypothesis, Helen. Why did you bring up the question of Dennis Gurton's almost-accident? You're not telling? At least tell us which of these items Malory listed is relevant, according to you."

"You think Helen knows who did it and why and isn't going to explain it to us? I don't believe it! Helen, do you?"

"I'm not sure. Or not sure enough. As I just said, there's too much I don't know. Das' disappearence, for one. Why wasn't he on that flight to India? I can't make it fit. Of course Clare's part in all this is not much of a mystery. And I think I'm beginning to have an inkling about who the murderer might be".

"And you won't tell us, is that it? Your nearest and dearest and we'll be the last to know," Alice teased.

I realized that actually she was put out that I wasn't more forthcoming. We haven't had to deal with such a situation before. Few of my jobs were interesting and even fewer were murders. The issue of solving a case did not arise very often.

"Could Das be dead? It seems to me that is a possibility. Perhaps he's also been murdered, just his body hasn't surfaced yet. What about that?" Nate broke the incipient tension between Alice and I.

"I agree, he could be dead. Perhaps down in that construction site. Except I bet the police checked it."

"Oh? Like they checked the model suite the first time out. Bet they didn't check it for Das' body. He's their prime candidate for murderer, not for victim," said Alice, as quick as ever. "If he isn't dead, where is he?"

"Right. Where indeed? I would have given odds he had every intention of going to India when I saw him that night. And Mel Romulu agrees. Something must have happened after I left ..."

I didn't like where this was taking me. Nate kept me on track.

"And that's no secret. What happened was the murder. Why are you two so sure he had no part in it? You're saying that the police picked him as the murderer because he's Indian? Maybe you are refusing to believe it for the same reason, eh?"

"Well, how about that! It's fair comment, but no, his origin is not the only reason the police are after him, and no, it's not the only reason I don't think he's involved. But I don't deny it's a factor. It's impossible to pin down the effect of a pro-and-con bias like that. It's definitely something to watch," I answered.

Alice drank her wine and said nothing.

The food came and we dug in. At least I did. Both Alice and Nate picked at theirs. Alice was still put out with me for not sharing my ideas about the case. That I could tell. As for Nate ... I didn't know.

The subject of murder was dropped. We talked about other things; the news from Europe, the constitutional mess here in Canada, the Juno Awards, music, movies, books, vacations. Nothing personal. Finally I did it.

"So what are you doing these days, Nate? And Ronnie? Is he still around?"

Innocent enough questions.

"Ronnie is dead. AIDS," Nate said and kept on eating. Then he looked up, put down his fork, and smiled at us. "How I hate doing this, always wait until the last possible moment. People don't know how to react to news like this, it casts such a pall. Well. I test positive for HIV. I don't have AIDS yet. Maybe I'll be lucky and get a couple of years before it gets bad. Ronnie went quickly; he died at Casey House Hospice exactly four months ago."

Nate was so right. We didn't know how to take it, how to react. What did I feel? What was appropriate? Was I feeling what was appropriate? Did it matter?

I put out my hand. He grasped it. I forced myself to look into his eyes. What had changed since he gave us the news just thirty seconds ago? It was still my sweet friend Nate, that had not changed. It was also a man under sentence of death. We are all going to die but no matter the banality of it, the when and how does make a difference.

"What a relief to have that out! Really, sometimes I think the hardest thing I've had to do since that test is telling people the results. Especially people I care for. Ronnie went so quickly I didn't have time to deal with his illness before he was gone. It was a shock, more like an accident, you know. Other friends ... My own ... situation I seem to be able to cope with.

So far. I don't really have any symptoms yet, so I'll have time to accept it when it comes. I didn't plan to hide it from you and I don't mind talking about it. Just so you know."

He let go of my hand. We both looked at Alice. She was crying quietly to herself.

"Oh, Nate! I'm so sorry! For Ronnie whom I never met but heard so much about and for you. It's so sad. Such a waste. A whole generation of gay men being decimated. And all those people in Africa and Haiti. People don't seem to think about it much until it touches them. It's so terrible."

"Yes. I hardly gave it a thought myself until Ronnie got sick. It was his death and my positive test that changed my awareness. But I think that's okay you know. It's not healthy to brood about illness and death. People shouldn't. I don't want to spend the rest of my life around people in sackcloth and ashes, wailing and grieving. That's not how I want to live, why should others?"

"You're very brave, Nate. I do so admire you!" Alice wiped her eyes and gave him a little smile. Nate went as if to pat her hand but didn't quite do it. Instead he returned to his plate and started to eat with a lot more appetite than before.

Alice had had her cry and felt better. She said, "Helen, did you see what was happening? Nate was comforting us! It's bizzare, isn't it. Nate, is this what happens every time?"

"Every time!"

We laughed together at the absurdity of it all. And had a great time for the rest of the evening.

▲

THERE WAS A LITTLE RED LIGHT on the message machine when Alice and I got back to her apartment. By common consent we left it alone and it continued to shine all night. Maybe it was for me with some news of the murder. Or from one of Alice's theatre friends. We didn't care, we had other things to think about.

Stepping out of our clothes, we plunged into bed. After a while, laying quietly in the crook of my arm, Alice said, "What d'you think, Helen?"

"About what?" I replied, although I knew what she meant. Alice understood my reluctance and, without showing any impatience, took the trouble to lead me.

"Nate and AIDS. Death, and all that. How does it make you feel?"

"You want the truth? Lucky, that's how. Sad, too, of course, but mostly lucky."

"Yes. Lucky. I feel so glad to be alive. Full of life. Doesn't seem right to feel like that."

"Yeah. Life means more. Just occurred to me that Ronnie is the first person I've known personally who's died of AIDS. Lots of dykes I know work in AIDS groups but I don't know any lesbian who has it. Most gay men have dozens of friends who have died or are sick. That's the part that's so ghastly. We have been fortunate, that's for sure."

"I really like him, you know. Nate. D'you think he would like it if I asked him over sometime? I'm going to be in a *Buddies in Bad Times* 'Queerculture' performance next week. I could get him tickets, hmm?"

"Nate would love it, I'm sure. Do I get invited, too, or what? And how come I hadn't heard about this 'Queerculture' gig of yours? What else are you keeping from me?"

We had barely touched the subject of AIDS, although much of the evening had centred around it. We had been unprepared and it was a shock. We do not live with AIDS. It was with relief that we now changed the subject. In that we differed very little from most people.

"I haven't kept anything from you, Helen! It just hadn't come up. Anyway, I only heard yesterday for sure. You're the one who's keeping things from me! About your murder case I mean, your solution. I want to know. Tell all!"

"I haven't got a solution, as you call it. Although it does feel like a crossword puzzle sometimes. I think I can guess who Clare's lover is, who helped her move the body."

"Who? Come on, Helen, tell!"

"You know everything I know. You figure it," I teased her.

"Bull! You were there, you've met all these people. Just hearing about it isn't the same at all."

"Okay, okay. I'll tell you what. How about I give you the name and only that. Then you figure out how I arrived at it. I don't have to answer any more questions. Deal?"

"Deal."

"Eleena DeMoulard."

"Seriously?"

"Yep."

"That's it then, eh?" said Alice.

I didn't bother answering but fell asleep leaving her wide awake, thinking.

In the morning we tried to avoid the red message light as long as we could. I was in the bathroom when Alice finally rewound the tape and listened. When I came out she was standing by the bureau grinning at me.

"Some coincidence. That was Eleena! She called at eleven last night to tell you that Clare Harwood had been arrested. She sounded upset, wants your help. You were right about them. Congratulations!"

▲

CLARE HARWOOD LIVED in a newish townhouse on a suburban cul-de-sac in Willowdale. It was one in a bank of houses each with about a six-metre frontage; three tiny bedrooms and a bathroom up; living, dining, kitchenette, and a two-piece down; a utility room and garage instead of a real basement.

It didn't take any deductive skill to figure out that she hadn't been here long and that the mortgage payments weren't easy to make. The furnishings were largely remnants of a long line of apartment living with just a few brand new pieces bought especially for this house.

Harwood's two teenage kids were still with her sister at the family cottage, so there were only the three of us in the house.

Eleena stood by the window, looking out at the scrap of a front yard and my dirty blue Escort parked behind her pretty little convertible. She was dressed in a dark green warm-up suit and she'd been crying. She kept bringing her hand up to her face as if brushing off stray hair. She hadn't given me a glance since I arrived.

Clare Harwood in jeans and sweater — more like the Clare I used to know years ago than the businesswoman who'd hired me — sat at the table with a cup of coffee in front of her.

"Morning, Helen! Coffee?" she asked. I just nodded and looked at the silent Eleena. Clare got up and moved towards the pot on the stove. It seemed like hours before she got back with a mug of coffee for me and broke the tension.

"Well, I'm glad you're here. Eleena wasn't sure you would come, you know — when you didn't call back after my arrest."

"I came as soon as I got the message this morning." I dismissed Eleena's paranoia about me. "So they let you go, I see. What was all that about?"

"The police claimed that you told Malory that I'd moved the body. That I told you what — "

"In confidence! What kind of a friend are you! You repeated to the police what Clare told you in confidence, as between friends. How could you!" Eleena's outburst interrupted Clare's careful speech.

"Do you believe I repeated what you told me about moving the body, all alone, to the police?" I turned to Clare.

"Not really. I figured they lied. I figured that you'd guessed about Eleena and me. You did, didn't you? Well, the police hadn't gotten onto that, so you couldn't have mentioned it to Malory. Probably they were just fishing. But I couldn't be sure, could I? They did take me downtown for questioning again."

"What did you expect? They'd established that the murder took place in the model suite and you insisted you'd been there. What did you tell them this time?"

"I didn't change my story one bit. They cannot prove that I wasn't alone, that Eleena was with me, that we found the body and moved it. Screw them, I'm not going to involve Eleena!"

"For heaven's sake! Not that dumb story again. I'm surprised they let you go. Did you sign anything to that effect?"

"No. I said I wouldn't say any more or sign anything without a lawyer. Later today I'm supposed to go there with my lawyer and make a proper deposition."

"That's a relief. That gives you one more opportunity to tell the truth. Take it."

Good for Malory, I thought. He doesn't think she's the killer. He just wants to give her a chance to come clean and not commit herself to another pack of lies.

"No! I won't bring Eleena into it! I cannot."

"You won't or you cannot?"

Eleena turned away from the window and moved towards Clare and I at the table. Her sharply etched silhouette dissolved as she came nearer. She seemed to have forgotten that she was mad at me.

"Helen, what shall I do? She refuses to tell the police the truth because of me. I know that all along it was me who wanted to keep it quiet that Clare and I were lovers. But now, I think it would be better if we admitted we were in that apartment together and found the body together and moved it together. We can support each other. Tell them exactly how it was. But she won't and she won't let me, either."

"I said no! You always told me that you and Mel were a couple for life. That you had no intention of breaking up with him. That it must never get out that we were lovers, lesbians! Those were your terms, remember? And I agreed. Well, now we must stick to it."

"But why? I don't understand why," Eleena cried, looking at me as if I had the answer. Clearly, the two of them had gone over this issue often in the past few days and disagreed. It no longer seemed worthwhile pursuing the discussion between them. They needed some fresh input, maybe a referee. If that was my role here, I had nothing useful to say.

"Why? I told you a thousand times! Because if we came out of the closet, it's the end of us. We'll probably never see each other again. I'll loose my job and Mel will make you swear not to see me again. On the other hand, if we just hunker down and wait it out, once it's all over we can continue as before. Damn it, Eleena, I don't want to loose you! Is that so hard to understand?"

"I'll leave Mel. I'll go with you. I said I'll do that. Just let's go to the police, tell them everything, and take the consequences!" Eleena now sounded really desperate. It was a sound that Clare knew.

"I cannot have you sacrificing yourself for me. What kind of relationship would we have after that? No! I just don't believe telling the truth would help me with the cops, but I know that it would ruin the most important relationship in my whole life. I cannot risk it."

"It wouldn't be a sacrifice, I promise. I want to live with you. Clare, I love you!"

For a second I saw that Clare was tempted. But she didn't let it sway her.

"You never said that to me before this happened. Why

should it be true now, all of a sudden? You always said you wanted an affair. Good time, no commitment. Okay, I went along. Why would Dennis Gurton's murder make any difference to the way you feel about me? It doesn't make sense. Please, sweetheart, let me handle the cops my way."

Clare spoke looking at Eleena so pleadingly, her face distorted by love and pain, that I wanted to flee. I hate feeling like a voyeur and I wasn't contributing anything to the resolution of their problem. I didn't know what I could do but I thought I had to try. Alice claims I have delusions about being able to fix things.

"Clare, tell me more about what the cops said. You must have gotten some idea of what their current theory is. Who do they think was your partner?"

"Oh, Nicky. They are all hyped up about Nicky. They found somebody who picked him up that night, I think in the garage, and they are sure it was about the same time that George saw me go down in the elevator. So they think we were together upstairs moving Dennis' body and then we split up. They think that Nick walked down the stairs all the way to the garage and I took the elevator to the second floor. That other detective, D'Arcy, tried to make out that someone saw us together, but nobody could have — Nick and I weren't together that evening! Those people who picked up Nick, whomever they are, didn't see me, couldn't have seen me at all."

Clare stopped, gave me an anguished look, and put her arms around Eleena who had started to cry. They held each other like two children lost in a storm. I tried not to let it distract me and continued to press Clare. I might as well take advantage of my hard-nosed rep, nothing would change it, anyway.

"How about the murder? Do the cops make you and Nick Das as the murderers? How do they explain you moving the body?"

"Oh, Helen! I don't know what the damn police really think, if they think at all. They kept trying to get me to say that I just helped Nicky because he was my lover. I guess they think he might have killed Dennis and then gotten me to help move the body. They seem comfortable with that idea. I don't understand why, they aren't very forthcoming, you know. It's all such nonsense!"

"It would help if you told the truth like Eleena, suggests."

"I don't see how. If I told them about me and Eleena, they might just switch to thinking it was me and her who killed Dennis rather than me and Nicky. She would be arrested and grilled like I was! And for what?"

Naturally, Clare saw the whole matter in the light of her personal situation. She wasn't concerned with solving the murder. That telling the police what really happened that night might help in finding the murderer was not a factor she chose to consider. It was hard to blame her. On the other hand there was Das. The police probably didn't have enough evidence to charge him, but if the killer wasn't found Nikhil Das would remain the prime suspect, would go through life with this hanging over his head. I didn't like it.

"Look, Clare, if you told the truth, it might at least take Nicky Das off the hook."

"But why should he be off the hook? He might have done it. We know nothing about what he did that night. You're asking me to sacrifice Eleena for Nick? Give me a break!"

She was angry and defensive. Full of the righteousness of love. There wasn't much to add to that. I left them sprawled on a sofa in each other's arms. I had been no help at all.

"YOU'RE DAMN RIGHT I think Harwood and Das did it!"

Malory was being vehement. We were in his office in the new pink and blue postmodernist police headquarters at College and Bay streets. I had gone directly there on leaving Clare's place just on the off chance that I could get to Malory. He was there and quite ready to see me.

"Why do I need to consider other possibilities for which I have not a scrap of evidence? I have a perfectly elegant solution. One, we know Clare Harwood was in that suite, that much she admits. Two, we found her fingerprint on the maintenance trolley. Just the one I admit; they wiped it pretty well, but it's physical evidence, and juries like that. Three, it took two people to move that body, it wasn't dragged, it was moved very carefully. She couldn't have done it alone. Four, Harwood was seen going down the elevator from the sixteenth floor at about the same time that Das was taking off from the garage, in a car with two friends of his. That's number five. These friends of his, we checked them out, they were clean. He'd arranged to have them pick him up that evening and to stay the night at their house. They drove him to the airport next morning to catch an early flight. According to them Das had instructed them to drive in directly to the garage, which wasn't open to visitors, told them he would be there to open the overhead door. They did that, he was there waiting for them with his baggage. He explained that this was quicker and easier than stopping at the main entrance. And that's why security never saw him leave. Enough for you?"

"No."

"What is it with you, Helen? I have the two people I need, I have circumstantial evidence, maybe not enough to convict as yet, but that's only a matter of time. And you really want me to go on looking for two extra people, another partner for Harwood *and* a separate murderer? Maybe you know who these mythical people are? Maybe you would like to tell me?"

"No."

"Well then."

"Well then, nothing. Have you found Das yet?" I couldn't resist rubbing it in that they hadn't been able to trace their prime suspect. I was in a cleft stick and it was unfair to take it out on Malory. It wasn't totally, or even mostly, his doing and I wasn't feeling very good about it.

"Oh," he said, very offhand, "forgot to tell you. Das did take that Air Canada flight, after all. And he did get to India. We've been trying to contact him in New Delhi at his sister's. Nobody's home. The local police promised to help but they have their hands full with their own troubles. Can't expect them to give this any priority. So D'Arcy might have to go to India to find Das."

D'Arcy in India. The idea didn't bear thinking about.

"You expect D'Arcy to bring Das back in handcuffs? Won't you need extradition papers?"

"We expect Mr. Nikhil Das to come back voluntarily to help us with our inquiries," Malory grinned at me.

"Then don't send D'Arcy. Nobody in their right mind would go voluntarily anywhere with that guy."

"Very funny. Don't take it so hard, Helen. Sorry your friend Clare is involved. But she is and that's that. As for Das, well, like I said before, if it's not him, then who? I am not stupid. Give me someone else, I'll investigate."

"Give you! Why should I give you the time of day, never mind do your job for you!"

I was quite ready to end this conversation. It was giving me heartburn. Then I remembered something to ask Malory.

"Say, how come you missed Das leaving on that flight? I thought you said he wasn't on it."

Malory had the grace to look embarrassed.

"Computer error. The seat assignments got screwed up or something. That's what they told us, anyway" he said.

I leaned back in my chair and laughed and laughed. "Computer error!" Lovely. It sure was the only thing I had to laugh about.

As I walked out of his office, still chortling to myself, not to be outdone, Malory asked, "That business in the lobby last night about Gurton's automobile accident. That was just you getting back at Mrs. Gurton, am I right? You don't have anything I should know about, do you?"

"No," I said, and felt better.

Leaving my car at a precious meter, I walked down Bay Street past the accumulation of fancy new high rises. Ignoring the magnetic force of the Eaton Centre to the east, I turned west to Dundas Street. A little way along and up a flight of stairs was the Sai Woo, a restaurant of some repute and long standing, which predates the new bustling Chinatowns of Toronto. It serves fine, basic Cantonese food and dim sum; the more fashionable Szechuan dishes on the menu are not especially recommended. Sai Woo creates the comfort food for people like me; tasty and familiar is what I come here for. I ordered a whole batch of dim sum and asked Bill to let me use the house phone, since the Saturday lunch crowd was monopolizing the public instrument. I dialled Clare's number, hoping they hadn't put the tape on and gone to bed. No. Clare answered almost immediately.

"Clare, it's me, Helen. No, no, don't worry I'm not going to try to persuade you to change your mind. At least not right now. All I want is a word with Eleena. Okay?"

"Oh, all right. But don't upset her. You're not exactly the sensitive type, she is." Clare raised her voice, "Lena, honey, Helen's on the phone. Want to speak with her? Okay ... Helen, she's coming."

"Helen, I'm here. What can I do for you?" Eleena's voice sounded much stronger, happier, with nary a trace of tears. Nothing there that a bout of lovemaking with Clare wouldn't fix, I thought, not without envy.

"A question. Don't ask me to explain, just answer. Is Mel Romulu gay? Was he involved with Nikhil Das?"

There was a moment of silence on the other end of the line, then laughter.

"No and no! Whatever gave you that idea? Is it because I'm Clare's lover but want to stay with Mel? No, Mel's not gay and therefore he's not involved with Nicky or any other man. He and I, well, we are very close, life companions you might say. He's not much for sex but we do fuck, occasionally. I told Clare, you know, I told her everything right from the start ..."

"Okay, okay, I don't need all the details. I'm not trying to

136

pry into your private life. Just want to make sure it's not true about Mel. Young Norm Dossler told the police that Mel and Nicky Das were gay lovers. Now, of course the police didn't pursue it because it didn't fit with their scenario about Clare and Nick."

"Well, it's not true. I don't know anything about Das, of course. He could be gay, although I doubt it. But about Norm Dossler, well, he's got a bit of a crush on me, so maybe he's just making trouble for Mel. Norm seems a bit disturbed lately. Maybe that explains it."

"Maybe. That's all the questions I've got. Keep your nerve, Eleena. And try to persuade Clare to come clean. It really would be the right thing to do."

"The right thing to do," Eleena repeated, "yes, I see, and I'll try, I don't promise I'll succeed. This Clare of mine is one stubborn woman." She sounded proud.

"Stubborn or not, she's in love with you. I bet you could get her to jump out the window for you if you put your mind to it," I said and Eleena laughed, pleased.

"All right, Helen. Bye."

"Bye."

I thanked Bill, went back to my table and half-a-dozen little wicker baskets of dim sum.

▲

DIAMOND PLAZA TOWERS was still there just as I had left it the night before. Feng was back on duty at the desk, along with Selena Amos presiding over a lobby full of Saturday-afternoon bustle. Elevators busily taking people on errands down to their cars and up again to their apartments, laden with shopping. The door leading to the squash courts, pool, sauna, equipment room, bike storage, and convenience store swinging open and banging shut with annoying frequency.

James Glendenning was in the manager's office, sitting forlornly behind Clare's desk. "Where is Tillion," I asked.

"Helen, I don't know and I don't care right now. I fired him and ordered him off the premises and he laughed at me. Told me that Rebecca Gurton recommended to LWO that he, Tillion, take over the 'investgation' of our Phase II property and that we would be hearing from him. We are being whipsawed by these two, it's going to cost us, I know it. And if that wasn't bad enough, from what I hear, our manager and our head of security are prime murder suspects as far as the police are concerned. Can you imagine! I can't believe the bad publicity this will create and just at the time when the condo market is cooling. I don't need this aggrevation."

Glendenning paused, took out a spotless handkerchief and wiped his forehead. I said nothing, and he ranted on.

"Until things settle down and we can replace our whole senior staff here, Clare Harwood and Das and Tillion, I am going to have to sit here and keep things running as best I can. I'm glad that you are here at least, very glad. There's been a lot of complaints from residents, not surprising really but unreasonable all the same. They are naturally upset and taking it out on us, me and the staff, what's left. I want you to make the rounds, go talk to people, reassure them. People have threatened to move out, to put their apartments on the market. We cannot have that, it will destroy future sales, Phase II ..."

"Yeah, Phase II. Is that dead or what?"

"God, I hope not! Why should it be? We have a valid option to buy it. Like I just told you, I know that Gurton woman and Tillion will jack up the price of that property, but we will get it all the same. We must. There isn't another property like that available in all Metro. We have to have it."

He was still sweating. I pressed on.

"Who's financing you? Where are you going to get the bread to pay for that property?"

"That's confidential."

"Let me guess. Dr. Melhior Romulu is your godfather. Thanks, so I'm right."

"I didn't say anything!"

"It's all right, I'll never tell, I promise. Since I already know this much, a little more won't hurt. How much is Romulu putting up?"

Glendenning looked at me dully.

"Enough."

"If Diamond Plaza Towers Corporation cannot meet its payments, Dr. Romulu will pick up the lot for a song. Am I right?"

"Oh, hell, yes! And I'll lose every cent I own. That's why we must keep our residents happy and buy that property and start building as soon as possible and sell those new condos ... Not easy at the best of times. And with no staff, Tillion and that Gurton woman plotting to shake us down, not to mention this murder, bad publicity ... "

"Will you take some advice? Yes? Well, first of all don't give up on Clare Harwood, she didn't kill anyone and could be back here working her tail off if you let her. Forget the cops, just call her and get her here. Second, forget about me, make Sam Feng head of security, he's certainly qualified and deserves it. Leave running this place and keeping people happy to them. Got that?"

"And what else?"

"Third, get off your duff, go up and talk to Romulu. I don't think he is all that pleased with how Rebecca Gurton and Wayne Tillion are taking advantage of Dennis Gurton's death. Maybe they don't have you over a barrel as much as you think. If anybody can think of a way to shaft these two beauties, it will be Mel Romulu. It just could be that he wouldn't enjoy profitting from any squeeze Gurton and Tillion put on you. Or from your troubles due to this murder. So he might help. It's worth a try."

"I don't know. Seems very unlikely to me." Glendenning gave me a speculative glance but sounded unconvinced.

"You got a better idea? Go ahead."

As I left, he was reaching for the phone. To call Clare and Feng and maybe even Mel Romulu.

I went up to Das' apartment. The cops had made some attempt to tidy it up so it wasn't actually trashed. But it felt used and abused all the same. I was glad Nick Das wasn't here to see it. I got a beer out of the refrigerator; the cops had left one in the six-pack, nice of them.

Should I leave this place right now? I had a feeling that my time at DP Towers was about over. If Glendenning had taken my advice, not only would Clare be back in harness shortly but Sam Feng would be getting the credit and the pay for my job, which he was doing anyway. All of which would make me seriously redundant — except as an investigator of the murder of Dennis Gurton. No matter how much I wanted out of there, I wanted to crack this case. Its ramifications interested me more and more. I would stay around for that.

I got a pencil and a pad of paper, sat down at Nicky's table, and tried to concentrate. First a list of names. I wrote them in a column down the left side of the page; everyone who had come up during the last five days since the murder, no matter in what capacity or connection. First, Dennis Gurton, the victim/murderee, and then the whole cast of characters/possible murderers — Rebecca Gurton, Wayne Tillion, Clare Harwood, Nick Das, Mel Romulu, Eleena DeMoulard, Joyce Dossler, Norman Dossler . . . not forgetting James Glendenning, George MacDonald, Sam Feng, and Selena Amos. I went down the list slowly one by one, noting alibis, trying to arrive at some convergence of time and place, some hidden pattern. Storybook detectives always manage to narrow the time of death and pin down the movement of suspects to within minutes. Not so here. According to Feng's report, no one noticed exactly when Dennis Gurton got in on the night of his death. So that was open-ended. Clare claimed to have found the body some time between ten and eleven. Virtually everyone on my list was either in the building — Clare, Nick, Sam, Selena — or came back into the building — Rebecca, Mel, Eleena, Joyce, Norm — during those evening hours. Malory had said that Wayne Tillion had an alibi of a sort. I wasn't sure what that meant but I crossed him off, anyway. He was a creep but that didn't necessarily qualify him for the part of murderer. I did the same for Rebecca Gurton. Sure, she was a crude opportunist, but I had seen her just after she saw the body and I didn't believe she killed her husband. She and Tillion wouldn't last long together. Sex isn't everything. Before the bed sheets needed changing they would be double-crossing each other over money. Good riddance. Then I crossed off Clare and Eleena. They didn't kill Gurton. Period. I had a side bet with myself that *had* they done so, their subsequent behaviour would have given them away. Anyway, some things you just have to take on faith. Could Glendenning have snuck in that night? Maybe, but it was such a long shot I couldn't bother with it. That left me with Nick, Sam, Selena, Mel, Joyce, and Norm. Down from twelve suspects to six. It was progress of sorts.

I scribbled and figured. Once on paper in black and white, some ideas I tried went into discard. One other started to gel. There was no evidence for it, naturally.

And, there was no more beer, either. A beer run was called for. It would do me good, flex my joints and clear the brain. I dropped everything and went downstairs.

I walked around the building to the parking lot, enjoying the scent of spring in the cool late-afternoon air. Days were perceptively longer now, something only northerners can fully appreciate. The long darkness of our winters is hard to take sometimes. More than anything it's the length of daylight which marks the ending of winter here. In southern Ontario the amount of daylight is a better indicator of changing seasons than temperature, which can vary widely.

By the time I found the nearest beer store, bought a twelve-pack of Brick Bock Ale in the traditional long brown bottles to celebrate spring, and drove back to the Towers, dusk was settling in. I was minding my own business, walking around my car towards the path leading to the front of the building with the case of beer under my arm, when something jogged my side and I almost dropped it. A bike had gone by me, the cyclist peddling like the devil was after him. There was a flash of a white face as he looked back to see who or what he'd almost run into, but he didn't slow down and in seconds was out of sight. I couldn't be sure who it was. Young, male, and expert on a bike is all I could deduce.

In the lobby things had settled down to a pre-dinner hush. Those who were going out for the evening were already gone, any guests had already arrived, and the late-night crowd was primping or laying down a happy-hour glow to take downtown.

Feng was on his break; I was pleased to hear he took them. I asked Selena about the mystery cyclist. She thought it might have been Norm Dossler's friend, Roy, last name unknown. They had been together a little while earlier but young Dossler had definitely gone up to his apartment alone and she hadn't seen him come back down. Perhaps after they'd parted Roy had stayed around outside in the parking lot to practise jumping curbs on his mountain bike. It wasn't permitted and both boys knew it. But what could you do? she asked rhetorically. What indeed, I sympathized, and made for the elevators.

With a fresh beer beside me I sat back to contemplate my shortened list of suspects. I took the easier ones first. Sam Feng. I had no motive for him but that was the least of my problems. If Feng was the murderer then Selena Amos had to be an accomplice. And vice versa. They had been on duty together that night, just like they were tonight. I thought of Feng being on a break that night. Could he have done it in that time? Selena had been sure that he wasn't out of her sight for more than five minutes at any one time. Both she and Feng claimed that he'd gone once to the can and once to the convenience store for a bottle of New York Seltzer to which he was heavily addicted. Selena had had her break at the desk. Coffee from the machine and a tuna-salad sandwich from home. Her two trips to the can during her shift were short and for the usual reasons only. Feng had confirmed the number and duration of her trips to the toilet if not the occasions. There is no way to disprove an alibi like this without an independent witness to contradict the story. There is no way to prove it, either. It's not watertight; like being miles away at the time of the murder, without the means of getting to the scene and visible to a whole bunch of other people. Sam and Selena alibied each other. This gave them every reason to support each other's story. It could even be true. I put question marks after their names.

So much for the easy part. What about Nick? He could have murdered Gurton, just like Clare had said. Since I was taking Clare's and Eleena's innocence on faith, why couldn't I take Nick's? He was absent and unknown. How much difference would it have made if he was around to tell his story? Some, but not enough. If I knew him better, could I take him on faith, like I did Clare and Eleena? No, it just wouldn't work and I had to accept that if I was to be honest with myself, and objective. Nikhil Das would stay on my list of suspects because I couldn't be sure that I understood him well enough.

I was certain that I could read Clare and Eleena but my arrogance couldn't stretch to cover Nick.

I sighed and turned to Mel. Here the possibilities seemed unlimited. There was no doubt in my mind that, unlike Clare and Eleena, Mel could have murdered Dennis Gurton and not given one sign of it since. He had "a sort of" motive, opportunity and the smarts to carry it off. In spite of this I didn't think he had killed Gurton. More arrogance on my part? Perhaps. I left him on the list.

What about Joyce Dossler? And young Norman. Roy(?), Joyce, and Norman. Joyce and Mel. Mel and Norman. Mel and Sam Feng(?) and Selena Amos(?). How many configurations like that could I come up with? I scrubbed the lot. Mel, Joyce, and Norman didn't need partners. Each one could have done for Gurton quite alone. Bad practice to introduce unnecessary elements, complications, into a solution. Inelegant. So I was left with Nick, Mel, Joyce, Norm, Sam and Selena.

I looked hard at the list of names and circled one of them. The phone rang. I picked it up on the first ring. There was no greeting, just Melhior Romulu's voice sounding quite cool.

"You sicced Glendenning on me."

It wasn't a question. I didn't answer. Silence grew for a second or two. Then Romulu sighed and continued, "I'm coming down to talk to you."

"Okay."

We hung up simultaneously. I opened another beer and waited. It took him six minutes to get there.

▲

FOR A CHANGE MELHIOR ROMULU came in wearing Levis and an unexceptional sport shirt. Mundane. He might have seemed quite ordinary had it not been for the grimness of his three-part face and the hostile awkwardness of his body. He took up a lot of space, both corporal and psychic, making the room and me, its sole inhabitant, seem small and insignificant. Without apparently trying to intimidate he was putting me on the defensive. A very different man from the good-natured host of our previous encounters.

"Have a beer," I ventured, "Spring Bock. Good stuff. Sorry, I don't have rye."

Romulu waved my offer aside.

"You sicced Glendenning on me," he repeated. I shrugged. "So?"

"What made you do that?"

"Is that what brings you here, to ask me that? Pretty obvious, isn't it?"

"How obvious?"

"Well, you set up the whole situation, didn't you? So it

146

seems only fair that you take a hand in resolving it. Don't you agree?"

"You accusing me of murdering Dennis Gurton?"

"Oh, come on! No, not directly, no. But you have been the deus ex machina in all of this Phase II property caper. I bet the soil contamination rumour came from you and you manipulated Joyce Dossler and then the Gurtons into moving to DP Towers. That's my guess."

It didn't faze him.

"Your guess? And what's your guess as to why I would have done all that?"

"For your amusement and potential profit."

Romulu silently considered my answer, meanwhile looking at me searchingly from under his mighty brows. But I had ceased to feel intimidated, at least momentarily. I knew I was on to something. After a moment Romulu grinned and seemed to relax.

"Yes, indeed. Amusement and potential profit. Quite good, very good in fact. It doesn't make me responsible for the murder of Dennis Gurton, now, does it?"

"Responsible?" I made a face. "Only in the sense that you created the situation which in turn generated the murder. No, my guess is that you bear no legal responsibility for the murder."

"Ah! But you are claiming that I bear moral responsibility for it."

"Moral?" Again I made a face. "Abstract morality is neither here nor there. There is nothing anyone can do about the death of Gurton and precious little about the murderer, either. But there is still an opportunity to help clear up some of the mess you made for other people."

"That's why you sicced Glendenning on me. You were

giving me a chance to mitigate the fall-out from my evil deeds. You're an arrogant woman, you know that, Helen!"

"It takes one to know one, Melhior."

He laughed.

"Well, my thanks, anyway. I guess I did need a prod. Here is what I did after Glendenning called me, as you advised him. First of all, I took over from the DP Towers Corporation their option to buy this blasted piece of land. That makes it my business directly. Then I called Rebecca Gurton and told her I intended to purchase that property immediately, without waiting for any assessment. Told her to get Tillion off the case. If she refuses or stalls any more, I'll get after her for conflict of interest, unprofessional conduct or whatever. At the very least, ruin her chances for a big-time career. This meet with your approval, so far?"

Nobody likes to be caught out. Romulu could try his damnedest to be gracious about it but he couldn't resist a dig or two at me. Ignore it, I thought, you're doing fine.

"And once you get the property what are you going to do with it? Resell it to Diamond Development Corporation at a serious profit?"

"You have something against profit?"

"Profit, shprofit. Depends how it's made. Flipping property and driving up the price of land and housing makes you a leech."

"How about driving the price *down* by claiming soil contamination and threatening an environmental assessment? Surely that that would be okay by you? And that's what I put in motion with Gurton and Life Watch Ontario, as you were sharp enough to figure out. Doesn't that make me a upstanding citizen?"

It was my turn to laugh.

"Nuts. Get serious. What if that soil really is contaminated, what then?"

Romulu managed to look pleased with himself.

"I can't tell a lie. It's not likely to have been contaminated; there was nothing on there in the last fifty years to produce hazardous waste. I have a contact in the Defence Department in Ottawa who checked it all out for me. You called it; it was a scam. And it worked."

"Your scam killed Dennis Gurton." I hated the way that sounded. But he let me get away with it.

"It had a bearing, yes, I admit that. To my honest regret."

"Since you say that you must know who the murderer is."

"Do you?"

"I don't know, there is no evidence, but ... "

I picked up the pad of paper with the names of suspects and passed it on to Romulu. He looked at it, noted the circled name, and nodded.

"Yes, I see. Most unfortunate. I never intended the thing to get so out of hand. I've had trouble sleeping ever since. Believe me —"

"Sure," I said dismissively.

Romulu put his large-knuckled hands flat on the table and leaned across it towards me. The move should have been threatening but somehow it didn't come over that way.

"All right. Nuff said. I wonder what the police think. Well, I'm on my way. It's been ... interesting talking to you. By the way, I understand from Glendenning that Sam Feng will be taking the security job over from you, at least until Nicky gets back. You'll be glad to leave, I expect. Goodbye."

He didn't offer to shake hands but straightened himself to

his full height and made for the door. To his back I said, "Yes, I'm glad about Feng. And Clare Harwood, she'll be back here very soon. The police won't be holding her now."

For a second Romulu froze in his tracks at the mention of Clare. Then he opened the door and without turning round to face me said goodbye again.

"Goodbye," I answered.

▲

AFTER MELHIOR ROMULU LEFT I doodled a bit, then dropped my pencil and walked out onto the little balcony to cool off. It had been a tense encounter in which more had been left unsaid than I liked. Between us we could have figured out what to do about the murderer, had we been less adversarial with each other. Nevertheless I had held up my end with Romulu. I had gotten through to him and that made me feel good. About time.

Standing on the balcony in the gathering darkness, I looked over the sculptured grounds of the Towers south in the direction of the neighbouring property which was the cause of so much grief all around. From this floor the junked buildings and debris with which it was strewn weren't visible.

What was visible was a light.

I stared at it for a long time, it didn't move or go out. It just flickered and glowed. It wasn't a flashlight or a lamp. It was a fire, small and controlled. Perhaps a bonfire. Perhaps a squat-

ter, a homeless person cooking supper. No way. I never heard of
the homeless in North York squatting on construction sites. It
just wasn't that sort of place. More likely kids. Could be a
wiener roast. Okay, it's Saturday night and the local mall rats
want a spot to party. A party with a little grass, a little coke, a
lot of booze, and a lot of sex. I didn't believe it for a moment.

The fire wasn't out of hand — yet. But it was on that Phase
II property in the jumble of decaying lumber, old tires,
wrecked sheds, abandoned barrels and who knows what. The
potential for a serious problem was there all right.

Someone was out there, someone had started the fire. Not
hard to guess who that someone was.

At the very least the situation called for the fire department to be notified immediately. And did I call 911 like any
responsible citizen? I did not. I was then and still am an
incurably nosy private investigator who likes to do things by
herself. To top it all, Romulu's visit had given my ego a boost.
I felt up for anything. Hubris.

I grabbed a flashlight from Das' well-equipped kitchen
closet and took the elevator downstairs, all the way down to
the basement, and let myself out the emergency exit. As I
pushed the door open I looked up at the electronic camera and
wondered whether Sam or Selena were watching on closed-
circuit TV. Well, this was one way to find out if they were on the
ball.

It was now quite dark and chilly. Walking past the parking lot towards the fence I shivered and wished I'd taken a
jacket. Then I figured that if the fire spread, cold was going to
be the least of my problems. Past the parking-area lights I
concentrated on following the pale flagstone path. There was
no gate through the wrought-iron fence which separated
Diamond Plaza Towers Phase I from the Phase II to-be.

Having long passed the stage of leaping tall buildings in a single bound or even medium-high fences, I looked around for a strategically placed piece of decorative rock to give me a leg up. Once over the fence I stopped and took a good hard look at the fire now glowing larger and more menacing in the gloom. This did nothing to improve my night vision, so I had no choice but to switch on the flashlight. Carefully following its bright yellow circle I moved maybe half-a-dozen steps in the direction of the fire, when a hysterical shriek froze me into panicked stillness.

"NNNOOO! ... NNNOO! ... NNO! ... NO!"

The desperate cry kept repeating, raising the hair on the back of my neck.

What was the appropriate response to a sound like that? Clearing my throat I tried "Hellooo," with a rising cadence, a couple of times and kept moving towards the voice. It was definitely coming from the vicinity of the fire. As I drew closer the cry turned into an evermore incomprehensible babble.

"NNO! GOOWAA! GOOWAAY! MEEN! GOOWAA! MEEN, MEEEN!"

A dark figure. It pranced about and waved its arms at me. Placed as it was between me and the fire, it remained unrecognizable, just a silhouette etched in sharp relief against the bright flames.

As I drew nearer, picking my way slowly, carefully over the treacherous terrain, the figure continued to stand its ground, becoming more and more agitated at my approach. The shrieks rose, a wall of sound projected at me as if to keep me back. It was then that I started to recognize some of the garbled words: "NO, NO! GO AWAY! GO AWAY! MINE! MINE!"

The rest was still just jabber.

The fire, which by now was blazing up a good three metres into the air, had been laid out in the middle of what had been the loading and turning area. What was left of the buildings clustered around this open space, fire reflecting on their façades, flickering eerily inside through broken doors and windows. From where I stood, the scene was of an amphitheatre with the fire and the shrieking figure as elements in a grotesque performance. An uneven but navigable path scraped clear by the backhoe led straight from beneath my feet to the centre of the stage set.

As I watched, momentarily mesmerized by the sight of the leaping creature, its cries became mixed with sobs. Sobs of the kind which come up from the pit of the belly, resonating through the diaphragm and chest, emerging in a spasm. Anybody who has ever sobbed like that will never forget it. Wracked with spasms the figure's head dropped, arms wrapped around the torso in a self-embrace, legs slowly giving away under the weight of what must have been unbearable pain.

I ran. Leaping over bits of broken pavement, I reached the collapsed figure and put my arms around the shaking shoulders. The face which turned to me full of anguish, bruised and black with soot, was that of Norman Dossler.

He stared at me through smoke and tears; it took him a moment to recognize who was holding him. For an instant his shaking body was still. Then with a wild yell he tore himself out of my arms and raced back towards the fire and the tangle of buildings behind. I stood up slowly, still winded from my run. Then the heat hit me. The fire was spreading.

Unnoticed, flames had crept along the ground from the

central core of the fire, moving from one piece of leftover combustible to the next, building up heat and intensity as they went. To my horror, balls of scorching flames leapt over intervening spaces and engulfed whatever remained of the buildings on the site.

Norman Dossler had disappeared into that inferno.

I didn't know what I could have done. It would be easy now to claim a quick response, a plunge into the smoke, a heroic deed. It didn't happen that way. Before I had time to decide, even to consider my chances of survival, never mind of rescuing Norman, he burst out of the centre of the conflagration, screaming and running in circles, his clothes ablaze. First he ran towards me, then almost back into the fire.

For the second time within minutes I scrambled towards him, calling ineffectually after him until he turned and threw himself at me. I was almost overpowered by a wall of dense acrid smoke and smell of burning flesh. Voiceless by now, he fought me for a second until all the breath went out of his wounded body; he gave up the struggle.

I wrapped my arms and as much of my body as possible around him and together we rolled on the ground, desperate to smother the flames which were burning him alive.

I don't know how long it took for the fire to give up. Not long, I guess. By the time good old Sam Feng arrived with a pathetic little fire extinguisher which he'd torn off the garage wall, and sprayed us with it, his efforts were redundant. Not that his arrival wasn't welcome; I'd never been more pleased to see another human being! And never more grateful for closed-circuit TV, alert security personnel, the North York Fire Department, Metro Toronto Ambulance Service, the burn unit at Toronto General Hospital ...

My burns turned out to be superficial, albeit painful

enough. Temporarily I lost some hair, one eyebrow, some skin from my hands. More permanently I ended up with a scar on my left breast, just where Norman's head had been pressed. It was a small, nasty burn which gave me trouble for weeks afterwards.

Norman Dossler suffered inmeasurably more. He lost one ear and much of his scalp; his hair never grew in properly again. There were burns on his arms and hands but the worst problem was with his feet. His expensive designer AIR runners turned into a trap. They proved highly combustible and hard to get off. As he ran through the burning debris, they almost crippled him for life.

But what I remember best were those moments before Feng's arrival when both Norman and I knew that he was safe, would live. For a few minutes we were alone face-to-face, rolled together on the hard ground, with the roar of the fire behind us, adrenaline still keeping the worst of pain at bay. Then young Norm opened his eyes, red and sore from the smoke and heat, and told me he had murdered Dennis Gurton.

Of course, I had guessed that already. And I had his name circled on my pad up in the apartment to prove it.

▲

I CAN'T REPRODUCE EXACTLY what he whispered to me then between spasms of tears and pain. It's all mixed up now with what came out later in the hospital and what we put together from other sources. Most of the elements of this pathetic story were in our hands all along.

Norman Dossler killed Dennis Gurton. That's the who-dunit. The rest was just details, mopping up. However Alice, among others, care as much for why and how, as for the simple who. So in subsequent days, bandaged and sore, I talked myself hoarse describing, explaining, repeating, and ultimately bull-shitting about the case, just out of sheer boredom with it all.

Norman Dossler, sixteen years old. He was a spoiled, screwed-up kid, with an authoritative father whom he idolized and a rather ineffectual mother whom he despised. His father's death shattered Norm's world. The house was sold, he and his mother had to move to an apartment, money became tight. Norman lost his dominant position with his teenage social group. It didn't matter that he was still better off than 99 percent of the world's adolescents. In his tiny world he'd lost status. He was desperately unhappy, insecure. According to his friend Roy, Norman had contemplated suicide even before the murder. Instead he killed Gurton, almost as a momentary substitute for his own death. Euphoria created by the murder, which he planned and executed perfectly, didn't last. The night of the fire he'd told Roy, after swearing him to secrecy, that he was going to kill himself. Roy was escaping from his demented friend when he ran into me at the parking lot. Athough badly spooked at the time, Roy kept his word and told no one.

Norman was totally obsessed with his father's legacy, the Phase II property with its derelict buildings. He set the fire, perhaps in defiance, perhaps as an SOS. When I arrived on the scene he was far gone, as close to total disintegration as I've ever seen anyone. I don't know whether my arrival saved his life; it hardly matters now.

But to go back. After his father's death and the move to DP Towers, the Phase II property had become for Norm a sacred inheritance, his only security, his one hope for the future. It would be sold, he would soon be a millionaire and once again the envy of his friends. Things might well have worked out very much like that except for the on-again off-again machinations between Dennis Gurton and the Diamond Development Corporation. Somewhere in all the goings-on, Norman got the idea that Gurton's environmental meddling would devalue the property or even prevent it from being sold for housing altogether. Wayne Tillion had let something slip about his job, about why he was at the Towers watching Gurton. It was the sort of boastful comment he might make to give himself status in the eyes of the affluent teenager. And to cut him down to size, perhaps.

After that Norm overheard conversations between his

mother and Melhior Romulu, whom he feared and disliked, which he took to confirm the danger that the Gurton investigation presented to his future. Norm wasn't alone in not seeing Romulu's hand in the whole deal. Moreover he was too naïve to understand that Gurton and DP Towers were merely dickering on the price for Gurton's cooperation. Rather, he took Gurton's commitment to environmental causes at face value. The danger of losing his inheritance was very real to him.

For Norman Dossler the choice lay between suicide and murder. This might seem extreme and even ridiculous, but then most of us don't live inside the skin of a disturbed sixteen-year-old boy. He decided to try murder. Suicide was always available as a way out if things didn't work out as planned. But first he would give Dennis Gurton one chance to escape his fate.

Accordingly he stationed himself at a corner up the street from the Towers and waited for Gurton to drive home from work. His intention was to talk Gurton out of blocking the sale of the property. It didn't seem to have occurred to him that Gurton might be late coming home that night or not want to talk to him. Maybe he didn't care. As it happened, Gurton came by only minutes after Norman had positioned himself at the corner. When Gurton's car halted for the stop sign, Norman cycled up the middle of the street towards him, stopped, and pounded on the driver's window just inches from Gurton's face. Dennis Gurton was not amused. He lowered his window, called young Dossler a few choice names, told him to get out of the way. All without letting Norman have his say. According to Norm, when he wouldn't move away from the car Gurton almost ran him down and in the mêlée hit a lamppost, denting his car's front fender. That was the minor accident I had seen the insurance adjustor investigating my first day on the job.

After that fiasco Dennis Gurton's fate was sealed. In a cold, selfrighteous fury, Norman Dossler planned Gurton's killing with care. When he thought about the murder, it was the planning he concentrated on, not the deed itself. I don't think he fully faced what he had done until it looked possible that he wouldn't get away with it. All during the investigation he had so successfully blocked any memory of the actual killing that even the fact that Gurton's body wasn't found in the spot where he'd died hadn't fazed him. Young Dossler didn't give himself away even to experienced interrogators like Malory. To them he appeared innocent because he didn't "act" innocent in the way they expected a guilty person might.

Then Norman heard me ask Rebecca Gurton about the accident, that scraped fender on Dennis Gurton's car. Suddenly the façade collapsed and he was overcome with fear and despair. This minor incident on the street had precipitated the murder. Its articulation aloud by others destroyed the false reality his unconcious had constructed for its own protection — at least, that's how the shrinks at the Clarke Institute of Psychiatry chose to decode these events after Norman's arrest.

The model suite was central to his plans. Someone like Clare with teenagers of her own should have figured out that a fully furnished model suite would be of interest to a teen living on the same floor. His fascination with it was heightened by the fact that 1606 was where Eleena, the woman of his adolescent dreams, was having clandestine meetings. Somehow he'd never twigged that she and Clare were in amorous dalliance. Probably it never occurred to him as a possibility. It was never established what he thought they were doing there. In any case he'd managed to acquire a key to it by the simple expedient of borrowing it for a few minutes from the door once when Clare forgot to remove it. Bold as brass, he took it downstairs and had a copy cut at the convenience store, then replaced it in the door before anyone was the wiser!

So much for the fun part. Now to cut a long sordid story short, on the night of the murder Norman Dossler stopped Dennis Gurton in the hall, apologized for the episode in the street and in his best conning-the-grown-ups manner, asked Gurton to describe the environmental assessment procedure. Then he inveigled Gurton into showing him the area in the Phase II property which was suspected of contamination. Their respective apartments didn't face the right way, so a window in the model suite was the natural choice for the show-and-tell. The door to it just happened to be unlocked; naturally since Norm had unlocked it.

According to Norman, after that it was easy. He and Gurton entered Apartment 1606, he told Gurton he was going to kill him, did so, walked out locking the door behind him and was in his own little bed in time to watch reruns of "Hill Street Blues." The whole thing took no more than ten minutes.

"You've got to hand it to the kid," I said to Alice. "He had it down to a *t*. No mess, no fuss, no bother. He was never seriously suspected."

"Don't sound so admiring, Helen. You don't fool me. I know you only do it to annoy. It's a ghastly story. His poor mother, how awful she must feel!"

Alice considered a moment and then asked, "How did he kill Gurton? What with?"

"Oh, that little mystery which has baffled our best and brightest forensic and detective minds. Well! Norm hit Dennis on the neck with his trusty Kryptonite lock! You know, you have one yourself. It's that U-shaped solid steel bike lock, every cyclist's protection against thieves. The ultimate environmentally friendly murder weapon for the nineties! How about that!"

Alice was speechless. But not for long. The next question I had been expecting.

"Helen, what's going to happen to him now? To Norm?"

"Who knows? It will depend on whether they find him fit to plead. That means sane enough to go to trial. Under our current Young Offenders Act, if he's found guilty he would be out in three years. If he's not fit to plead, he could be institutionalized for years, maybe forever. I expect the Crown will work to have him committed and his defence attorney will want a trial. That's the way it is."

"Institutionalized for years, that doesn't bear thinking about! On the other hand, I don't want him on the street at nineteen, either. What a choice! Is there no other way?"

"Hey, take it easy! Don't let it get you. Actually, I don't think he would be any risk on the street. His kind is more a danger to family, friends, and business relations. Anybody who stands in his light. That's what this was about. Look, Alice, it's not our decision, thank goodness. Forget it."

"Yes, but —"

"No buts. So where are we meeting Nate for dinner this time? Let's go, I'm starved."

We met Nate at The Boulevard Cafe. By then it was warm enough for service at the sidewalk tables. Trees along the side streets were popping their greenery like mad, my hands were healed so I could eat like a civilized human being, and I would have preferred to forget about Norman Dossler and DP Towers. Neither Alice nor Nate would let me.

"I'm not really clear about Melhior Romulu's part in all this." Nate put the ball back in play almost as soon as the three of us sat down.

"Welcome to the club. I'm not real clear how it all went down, either. He hasn't had to explain anything, there is no direct connection between his schemes and the murder."

"But how about that conversation you had with him just before the fire? Obviously he believed you knew what he'd been up to! So what was it?"

"Oh, I think I have the outline, but the nitty-gritty I guess we'll never know for sure. The way I read it, Mel is like a frustrated film producer. Just making money, especially in real estate, is too dull. He likes a little fun with it on the side. He saw the potential for having both in the DP Towers situation. Their shaky financial position, the possibilities inherent in the property next door under probate after Dossler Senior's death. My bet is that the idea came to him when he realized that Rebecca Gurton, who was the trustee in Dossler's will, was the wife of Dennis Gurton, the environmental lawyer for LWO. Remember both he and Eleena were members of LWO. Unlike most members of environmental organizations, Mel took the trouble to become familiar with the staff, the officers, and all of its projects. Somehow he manoeuvred Joyce Dossler into moving to DP Towers, probably by offering to lend her money to buy the condo. After that it would be easy to get the Gurtons to follow suit in order to be close both to Joyce Dossler and the property. Apparently it's worth something like twelve million dollars, imagine that! I don't know whether he suggested to Glendenning that Tillion be hired to keep an eye on Dennis Gurton, but I wouldn't put it past him. In any case, he had the whole cast of characters right under his hand.

"The financial permutations are over my head, but essentially he managed to get himself into a 'tails I win,/heads they lose' position. The crux of it was the financing for Phase II. He was Glendenning's only hope of capital as long as the property was suspected of having been contaminated by toxic waste or whatever. Nobody else would invest or lend a cent. But what if the whole soil contamination scare was a scam? Which ever way it fell, Mel Romulu could pick up the pieces. Like I said at that time, 'for his amusement and potential profit' — he didn't deny it. That's all I know. Enough already."

"He was really rich; the others weren't. He could have the fun of watching them squabble over that property and then just move in and take it."

As usual, Alice managed to cut through to the essentials.

"And it's not past tense, Alice. He's still rich, richer than ever now, I bet." I put in my two-cents worth.

"But how about Eleena? Did he lose her? That would be only just."

"Well, that's debatable. She hasn't left him as far as I know. But then she's still seeing Clare — on the side. And he is choosing to pretend not to know about it. How long can that kind of a situation last, would you say?"

Alice nodded at my hypothetical question, then went on following her own train of thought.

"You kind of liked Melhior Romulu, didn't you Helen? Right from the start. How do you feel about him now? He created the situation which drove Norman Dossler to kill Gurton; he's likely to make a lot of money on the Phase II property. And he's liable sooner or later to try to get even with

Clare Harwood for daring to take Eleena away from him. Nice guy, eh?" she said.

Before I could answer Nate smiled at Alice and said:

"Ain't that the truth. He reminds me of me, you know, Alice, as I was when Helen met me. That's just the kind of guy Helen would kind of like. And about the profit motive — you've got to understand that making money can be made to justify almost anything you do. Things which would be considered perverse if you did them just for kicks or as a hobby. Prove that the motive was profit and you're a regular citizen. See?"

Alice shook her head. She understood but didn't want to.

"As for him taking it out on Clare, I doubt it. Sounds to me like a man who can take his lumps. What d'you think, Helen?" Nate continued.

"Just like you, Nate, a heart of gold under a sleazy exterior," I kidded. Refusing to get suckered into the topic any more, I changed the subject. "Enough on Romulu. Now, which of you will have the honour of taking me to the airport next Friday?"

The night before, Alice and I had discussed our future together and agreed that we didn't have any. Alice was all set on an acting career in Toronto, she wasn't about to leave. And she understood that I didn't want to stay around the city after this. So that was that.

"We tossed for it and I lost, so I guess it's me. And Alice insists on coming along for the ride."

Wineglass in hand, Nate looked at Alice and me over his bifocals.

"A toast. To us."

We clicked glasses in silence. There was a small lull in the conversation as we started in on our meal.

"Whatever happened to this Indian guy you two were so worked up about? Remember? Nicky Das was it?" asked Nate.

So I told them what happened when I returned to DP Towers from the hospital to collect my things.

I walked in the door of Apartment 211 in Diamond Plaza Towers, eager and anxious to get out of there. Downstairs one of the staff had handed me a note which read "Please call a.s.a.p." and a number with area code 9111. Looked more like an emergency number than an area code. Clumsy with my bandaged hand, I punched it in anyway. After some heavy international buzzing, someone at the other end said:

"Hello, Helen Keremos? This is Nikhil Das. Nick."

My hand on the phone tightened involuntarily until it hurt. There was a second of silence, then I let out my breath and proceeded with the customary inanities.

"Hello, Nick. Good to hear from you."

"Yes, I understand you've had some trouble at the Towers. I'm really sorry about that. Terrible news about Dennis Gurton, terrible. Hope it's been sorted out. Has it?"

"You could say that, yes. We've been looking for you for a week. Where were you?"

He obviously had no idea how close he'd come to having his name on a murder warrant. I wasn't about to tell him!

"Oh, after her husband's funeral I took my sister and her children away to some relatives in the country for a few days. Their phone was on the blink and naturally there was no Canadian news. We just got back to Delhi yesterday and found all those messages from the Toronto police. I phoned right away but of course, because of the ten hours difference, it took some time before I could get Sergeant Malory, the officer in charge. After that, police here took my affidavit and we faxed it to Toronto. I just spoke to Malory again, and apparently everything has been clarified, so I don't have to come back to Canada right away."

"Good"

"Helen, I know it must have created a great deal of extra work and inconvenience for you. It's most regrettable indeed that due to my absence you had to cope with a situation you couldn't possibly have expected. I do hope Feng has been helpful."

"I don't know what I would have done without him. He certainly watches those monitors."

It had been Feng who saw me leave via that emergency exit, came out to check, saw the fire, and called the fire department. But I wasn't going to tell Das any of that, either.

"Good, good, I'm recommending to Mr. Glendenning that Feng replace me ... oh, unless you would like the job on a permanent basis?"

"No, not at all. Great idea. But aren't you coming back?"

"Well, no. I decided to stay in India, try to make a go of it here. For a while, anyway. My things can be sent over. I am sure Clare will arrange it for me."

Even across half the world I could hear the tension and hesitation in his voice. It hadn't been an easy decision to make.

"I have things to work out with my father ... and ... it's better I do it now."

"Well, good for you. And good luck, Nick."

"Thank you. Would you give my best to Dr. Romulu? Tell

166

him I miss our chess games. I'm obliged to you, Helen, thank you again."

"Not at all. Thank you. Goodbye."

"Goodbye."

I put the phone down and finished packing. I was out of there!

▲

THAT'S WHAT I TOLD ALICE AND NATE at our farewell meal at the Boulevard. I debated whether to leave out that last bit, the friendship between Nikhil Das and Melhior Romulu. Alice still has illusions about clear distinctions between bad guys and good guys. In the end I told it like it was.

Two days later the three of us stood awkwardly in front of the Passengers Only door in Terminal II at Toronto International Airport. Alice held on to me with one hand and to Nate Ottoline with the other. She wasn't quite crying but it wouldn't take much. They had both hugged me, we'd all promised to keep in touch, Nate to call, Alice to visit.

"I'll look after her, Helen, I promise." Nate looked sternly down at Alice.

"And I'll look after him."

"Well, bully for you two! And what about me? I guess I'll just have to look after myself!" I said, walking happily towards my Vancouver-bound Air Canada plane.